Becka
Defined

Becka Defined

A Child of God

Ann Szasz

ARCHWAY PUBLISHING

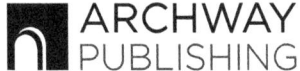

Copyright © 2018 Ann Szasz.

All rights reserved. No part of this book may be used or reproduced by any means, graphic, electronic, or mechanical, including photocopying, recording, taping or by any information storage retrieval system without the written permission of the author except in the case of brief quotations embodied in critical articles and reviews.

All scripture quotations are from the Authorized King James Version. This would have been the predominant version available to these characters in 1956. *The Holy Bible, Authorized King James Version,* Chicago, Illinois: Consolidated Book Publishers, 1950

This is a work of fiction. All of the characters, names, incidents, organizations, and dialogue in this novel are either the products of the author's imagination or are used fictitiously.

Archway Publishing books may be ordered through booksellers or by contacting:

Archway Publishing
1663 Liberty Drive
Bloomington, IN 47403
www.archwaypublishing.com
1 (888) 242-5904

Because of the dynamic nature of the Internet, any web addresses or links contained in this book may have changed since publication and may no longer be valid. The views expressed in this work are solely those of the author and do not necessarily reflect the views of the publisher, and the publisher hereby disclaims any responsibility for them.

Any people depicted in stock imagery provided by Getty Images are models, and such images are being used for illustrative purposes only. Certain stock imagery © Getty Images.

ISBN: 978-1-4808-6142-8 (sc)
ISBN: 978-1-4808-6140-4 (hc)
ISBN: 978-1-4808-6141-1 (e)

Library of Congress Control Number: 2018906551

Print information available on the last page.

Archway Publishing rev. date: 6/28/2018

This book is dedicated to my mother
Alma Lee
whose faith in God inspired me
and whose love and encouragement sustained me.

ACKNOWLEDGMENTS

Thank you to my dear husband, Frank, for enduring the hours that I was unavailable to him as I got lost in the creative process; cluttering the kitchen table with notebooks and pencils, laptop and Bible, reference books and inspirational materials.

I would like to offer my deepest thanks to my good friend Mary Ann Lutzenhiser for her honest and precious feedback during the writing of the book. She has a gentle way of providing correction and thought provoking questions that helped me more than she knows. Her excitement over the story kept me pressing on to the end.

Thank you, as well to my editor, Kimberlee Medicine Horn Jackson, MFA., MA., for believing in the merit of the message of the book. She has provided invaluable instruction and encouragement with kindness and grace. She took on a raw manuscript and showed me how to clean it up, polish it, and make it a more enjoyable read.

CHAPTER 1
Willa

April 1956

"Dr. Aldridge, emergency room, STAT." My name echoing off the walls continued to startle and thrill me after almost three years, particularly being called Doctor. The page was repeated two more times, but I was already running down the stairs before the second page was called. Only two female pediatric residents worked at Cincinnati Children's Hospital that year, and I was the one on duty that night. Dr. Fisher, the attending in ER, made no secret of his opinion of female physicians. The page likely meant some minor or nuisance case came in that he thought beneath him. I expected to be disappointed.

As I rounded the corner, I caught a glimpse of Nurse Wade sprinting to the supply room. She shook her head as she ran by me. "Two, doctor," she said, telling me where I needed to go. Her starched white uniform and thick white stockings made a symphony of shushing and riffing noises as she ran past me.

I knew something was up. I could hear Dr. Fisher's agitated voice screaming a few choice expletives. Behind the curtain, Len, the orderly, yelled, "Follow me, ma'am, so that the doctor can do his job."

Entering the split in the curtain, I witnessed chaos. Len attempted to corral a hysterical woman out of the area; Dr. Fisher and nurse Bell worked quickly and quietly on a young girl on the table. The child was moaning but still.

"Aldridge, this child has been severely beaten. She has facial fractures; we'll know more when we see x-rays. She has a head injury." And then he added just above a whisper, "And she's been raped."

I fixated upon the bruises and dark caked-on blood covering the child's knees and inner thighs.

"No, I told you…she fell off her bicycle," the woman screamed.

"Get her out of here," Dr. Fisher yelled as he continued suctioning the child's nose and mouth so she would not choke on her own blood.

Len took the woman by her shoulders and firmly walked her out of the area.

Dr. Fisher thrust the suction catheter toward Bell instructing her to continue suctioning, while he washed the blood from the girl's eyes and face. I jumped in and checked her blood pressure and heart rate.

"BP is seventy over thirty-two, heart rate one fifty six." The numbers indicated that the child was in shock. I raised her feet to increase blood flow by gravity toward her heart and lungs and started an IV in her arm. "How old is she?" I asked.

"Twelve," Bell said.

Thumping her wrists and knees with the rubber reflex hammer elicited a slight jump response from the girl. "Reflexes are good," I told him.

Fisher attempted to check her pupils. "The right responds,

but the left, well, the orbit is fractured," he uttered in frustration.

"Can you hear me?" I said softly in her ear, interrupting Fisher. I didn't want him to scare her if she was conscious. She responded slightly.

"Uh-huh," she moaned.

"I am Dr. Rebecca. What's your name?"

"Willa," she spoke clearly

"Do you know where you are?" I asked.

"At the hospital?" she asked. Still she did not try to move or open her eyes.

"You are safe here, Willa. Dr. Fisher and I are going to take good care of you. Nurse Bell and Nurse Wade are wonderful nurses. They will be very gentle. Okay?"

"Okay," she answered.

"Will you tell me what happened to you?" I whispered near her ear.

"Is mama here?" Her voice was shrill, fearful.

"Is that your mother who brought you here?" Dr. Fisher asked harshly. He was clearly angry.

"Mama!" Willa called out in her weak voice.

"Your mama's just outside. We'll let her come back in in a little while," I said. Dr. Fisher scowled at me.

I motioned for him to follow me to the corner, out of earshot of the girl.

"She's not afraid of her mother. Mother didn't do this," I asserted.

"But she's covering. She's lying about what happened." He could hardly contain his contempt.

"Clearly," I said calmly. "We will get to the truth."

Dr. Fisher pursed his lips and he scratched his high forehead; he barked orders to nurse Bell. "Check her blood pressure again and call x-ray," he commanded Nurse Wade, who had returned with more gauze, more saline, and some instrument packs.

This was the middle of a seventy-two hour on-call shift at the hospital, and sleep was a luxury that had not been afforded to me the night before. The respiratory ward was busy with children with pneumonia, whooping cough, and croup. In my sleep-deprived state, I was more aggressive instead of adopting my usual submissive manner with the senior physician. I was determined that he would not perform a pelvic exam on this twelve year-old girl while she was awake. He most certainly could have overruled me, but he backed down. We sent some blood work and prepared to transfuse the child. She was more stable, and so he left "room two" to check on other patients. The area got quiet; disturbed only by Willa's slightly labored breathing. The mother needed to come back and help keep Willa calm. We would also need her permission to transfuse and possibly do a pelvic exam under sedation. Willa screamed and drew up her legs when Wade tried to wash the blood from them. She was near frightened to death with all that was going on.

"Willa, we're going to bring your mother back now," I said, "but when we do, we have to wash the blood off your legs." I stopped for her reaction, but she said nothing. "And between your legs." I stopped again. Willa did not move or open her unaffected eye, and the left eye was now too swollen to open.

"Your mother can stay right here when we clean you up. Is that Okay?"

"Yes," she whispered.

While Dr. Fisher was clearly irate and laid blame on Willa's mother, I wasn't sure how to feel. I walked out to get her mother.

Like a shock wave, my mind was transported back to North Carolina 1939. My racing heart pounded heavy and tight in my chest. My mouth was so dry that air caught in my throat. Trembling and weak in the knees, I sidled over to a bench in the waiting area and sat down. Leaning forward I put my head between my knees.

Twelve years old! Twelve years old! I thought over and over again.

Nurse Cramer saw me sit down and hurried over. "Doctor, are you alright?" she spoke with genuine concern in her voice.

"I'll be fine, Cramer."

She brought me water in a paper cup from the cooler. "You're awfully pale, Rebecca," she said quietly. It was a breach of etiquette to call doctors by first name, but we had experienced many long nights in the ER and the wards. Sophie Cramer was the closest I had to a friend in Cincinnati. The cool water was soothing. Comforting.

"I can't do this," I said "I can't loaf off. I still have sixteen hours to go."

"Is it the little girl? Len told me"

"Well, I can't help her if I let it get to me. I'm okay now. Thank you for the water, Sophie," I got up, stronger now, but still shaky. I went to fetch the mother.

Just then, Wade came out quickly. "We need you back in there, doctor. She's hemorrhaging."

It still amazes me how a team can focus and accomplish objectives when a crisis arises. Len brought the mother back in. With permission, we anesthetized and transfused the girl, stopped the bleeding, repaired lacerations, and casted her arm with blinding speed and efficiency. The excessive pressure around her left eye caused a rupture of the orbit and necessitated removal of the eye itself.

Once she was stable, the hard work began; the physical and emotional healing. The latter being the more challenging.

While Willa slept I took the mother into a quiet room. Her mother was informed of all that had been done and that for the moment she was stable. "However," I explained, "her vaginal lacerations were severe. There is a strong risk of infection. She will, most likely, never be able to have children later on," I stopped to let her take in the news. She remained silent. Tears were running down her cheeks.

"Mrs. Lockhart, Willa has suffered a lot of trauma. Even if she recovers physically, which I think she will, the mental and emotional injuries may never heal if they are not addressed. Please tell me what happened. Who beat and raped Willa?"

She shook her head and took a deep breath, ready to continue denying the obvious. I stopped her before she could.

"This was not a bicycle accident. She won't be able to look in the mirror and not remember this awful thing over and over again. All of her life! And you, too, when you look at her, I know you want to help her."

She looked at the floor.

"I know you love her."

She wept.

Without another word about it, I put my hand on hers. She remained silent on the subject.

At the end of my seventy-two hours, I went home to my small apartment. It was seven am. Although it was my tendency to stay awake to review disturbing or troublesome events, I did not this day. I fell onto my bed; I did not eat; I did not bathe, but dropped off to sleep and slept straight from seven-thirty am to three o'clock in the morning. I was grateful that it was a dreamless sleep.

However, Willa was the only thing on my mind when I woke up. Reviewing all possible treatments, medications, IV fluids in my mind, I wondered, did we do everything? A litany of what we needed to check and tests to be done scrolled through my mind. Maybe I shouldn't wait to contact Dr. Cliff, Willa's attending doctor. I called and left a message for Dr. Cliff, asking him to call me when he had an opportunity. Meantime, Sophie filled me in over the telephone on all the children on my case load, especially Willa. The girl was not speaking to anyone, not even her mother, although she was awake. She would not eat. She took her medicine and her shots without resistance. Dr. Cliff was a competent and compassionate pediatrician. He could be trusted. It was difficult to let go, but I was not scheduled to return for another thirty-six hours. There was nothing to do but wait.

Memories enveloped me again; it was 1939, Belmont, North Carolina. I was twelve years old that summer, and the only girl of four children. I saw Papa's beautiful face as he preached behind the pulpit. He was so wonderful. He sang and praised the Lord with abandon. His joy was contagious.

Why did Papa love the Lord so much? He had suffered all his life with pain, with loss, with rejection. I tried hard to remember what he said when he preached. I could clearly picture him in my mind - a picture of happiness and contentment but I could not remember what he had to say about God.

Then a chill ran through me, worse than any Ohio winter. God! I felt bitter resentment. Anger at God! *Why am I so angry with God and my father is not angry with God?* I wondered.

I was three-years-old when mama died while giving birth to Benji. I couldn't remember her face, only the image of her in a photograph. Benji was mentally retarded as a result of the difficult labor mama went through to bring him into the world. He was one of the joys of my life. I wasn't angry with God for those things but Papa should have been. Papa's mother was murdered and he witnessed it. He should have been angry about that. He lost his first wife during the first war. He should have been angry about that. He lost his leg in the war. What about that? We lost Gammy, mama's mother and then Pappy, mama's father. Papa was very close to both of them.

Later, when my brother Aaron died at the beginning of WWII, and Benji died when he was twenty-two, that should have been the last straw. God had punished us enough. Papa's faith was strong; instead of anger, he praised God for his two remaining children, me and Matt and his daughter-in-law, and his grandchildren.

I had no use for God.

I know why 1939 kept returning to my head but I felt sick, cold and scared, and I tried to put it out of my mind.

CHAPTER TWO
Lorelei

Dr. Cliff telephoned me a few hours later to update me on the progress of several children. Willa had not had a very good night. She hadn't slept well and when she did she woke up screaming, but was still not talking to anyone, not even her mother. Staying away from the hospital was difficult for me.

There was nothing to do on a Sunday except go to a baseball game or the zoo. A baseball game was out of the question. I had gone to the zoo so often that I was beginning to lose interest. Instead I opted to write some letters and do some mending. My cello was calling me but I worried about disturbing the neighbors and so I neglected her. If there was one dream I had, after opening my own practice, it was to buy a house that had enough land around it that my cello could have her voice often and unrestrained.

Pleasant memories of my father's house and the joyous music that was played there entertained me. Hymns, classical music, popular and show tunes and even reels and bluegrass enlivened my father's house at almost any time. Papa had insisted that we each learn to play at least one instrument. Even

Benji was encouraged to bang on a pot or a tambourine to be a part of the activity. Papa first taught each of us to play the piano and then guitar, then he taught me violin and pan-flute. But it was the sweet, sorrowful sounds of the cello with which I fell in love when I was thirteen. When Lorelei came to live with us as Aaron's wife in 1941, Papa taught her to play the piano.

 Sweet Lorelei. I had thought of her as nothing more than a dullard when Aaron started keeping company with her. She was so shy and withdrawn that the term "wallflower" didn't even begin to describe her. She was skinny and wore tattered worn-out dresses. Her dirty reddish blonde hair was scraggly and long. I couldn't tell what her face looked like back then since she never looked anyone in the eye. She only looked up into Aaron's face. Maybe that pitiful, mooning look she gave Aaron was why I instantly didn't like her. She was taking my big brother away from me, but, I soon learned why she had such low self-esteem.

 One day, Aaron roared up to the house in his pick-up truck. He jumped out of the truck and ran in the house to talk to Papa. I was on the porch entertaining Benji and paid little attention to Aaron's urgency. He was dramatic now and then for, what I considered, little to no reason. I noticed someone sitting in the front seat of his truck and walked over to see who was there.

 She was hunched over in the passenger seat of the truck and her tangled strawberry blond hair was easily recognizable.

 I said hi, but she did not answer.

 "How are you Lorelei?" I tried again, but she still did not answer. She was making a soft, sniffing sound and I knew she was crying. "Are you okay?" I asked.

 About that time Papa, Aaron and Matthew came hurrying out of the house. "'Scuse me, baby" Papa said to me as he gently moved me out of his way. He opened the door and lifted little Lorelei out of the truck. Her face was beaten and swollen and her head dropped back. The sleeve and waist of her dress were torn. She was in bad shape.

"Let me take her, Papa," Aaron said and took her from Papa's arms. She reached around Aaron's neck and wept softly, clinging tightly to him with one arm, but kept the other arm close to her chest. Aaron's face changed when he looked so lovingly at her. His angular jaw and cheekbones seemed softer, and his sad smile more tender. "You'll be alright," he told her.

"Matthew, go and see if Dr. Stanton can come over here. He may be seeing people in his office, so just ask if he can come over when he has a chance," Papa said.

Matthew, my middle brother, took off running.

"What happened?" I asked Aaron. But he was clearly too focused on the hurt young girl to pay attention to his prying little sister. When he laid her down gingerly on the bed in Papa's room, she winched in pain. There were bloody scratches and fresh bruises on her arms, legs and face.

"What happened, Papa?" I turned to Papa knowing that he wouldn't ignore me like Aaron.

"I don't know, Sugar pie. Someone caused this child harm. But we're gonna take good care of her. Now, go make sure Benji is okay out there. He's getting all excited."

Benji, safely restrained in his wheelchair, was kicking and making his grunting noises, sticking his tongue out. "She'll be alright Benji. Papa will take care of her," I reassured him and stroked his head. He soon calmed down and nodded his head in acknowledgement. We both knew Papa could always make things right. Most things.

Dr. Stanton came along about supper time. Lorelei had been sleeping for a few hours by that time. Because it was a Wednesday, Mrs. Burton, one of the church ladies had come by to help me start supper and had also sat by Lorelei for a little while. Mrs. Burton could be trusted. She was not a gossip like some of the church ladies.

We invited her and Dr. Stanton to stay and eat with us. Mrs. Burton, as always, declined and said she had to get home to eat with her own family. Dr. Stanton also said no. After Mrs. Burton left, Dr. Stanton stayed to talk to Papa and Aaron. Matthew and I set the table and eavesdropped on the conversation. Dr. Stanton knew that I wanted to become a doctor and he encouraged me. Sometimes, he would take time to teach me about anatomy and medicine. I was hoping he would include me then.

"Her left arm is fractured at the humerus," he looked up at me and I pointed to my upper arm. He nodded in my direction. "It's a pretty bad break. I reset it, Jesse," he said to my father. "She has a concussion as well, but there is nothing that won't heal," he spoke with confidence.

"She's pregnant, Doctor. Do you think the baby will be okay?" Aaron asked him.

The doctor looked a little surprised at Aaron's revelation, but Papa did not. Aaron likely had told him at some point maybe even when he ran into the house.

Dr. Stanton puckered his lips and lowered his eyebrows and scratched behind his ear. Then after some thought said, "I think I'll go and check her again. I wish you had told me that to start with." He admonished Aaron. "Who did this to her? We should tell the sheriff."

"Her father. She told him we are getting married and he just started beatin' on her," Aaron raged.

Now it was Papa who looked a little surprised.

"Are you getting married?" Dr. Stanton asked.

"Yes. We want to get married"

Dr. Stanton responded, "You've got things a little backwards, son. You get married first and then produce children," he paused a minute. Aaron didn't say anything. "This isn't the first time he's beaten her," Dr. Stanton continued "I will let the sheriff know when I go back into town," he said and went back into the bedroom.

"I'm thinking her father will not consent to this marriage. Is she of age?" Papa asked.

"She's sixteen. We can get married without his consent," he answered Papa.

"Where are you going to live, son?" Papa asked.

So began our life with Lorelei in our home. She didn't lose the baby. They were married immediately. Aaron was eighteen at the time and as soon as he graduated from high school he joined the army. It was 1942. He was killed before his son, Paul, was born. Lorelei became my sister and love grew between us. She was a gentle spirit, kind and loving. She did not like herself and felt undeserving of Papa's kindness. Because of that she worked very hard to earn her keep at our house. Papa tried to convince her that her membership into the family was unconditional, but she worked from morning to night none-the-less.

She had struggled in school all along and so she wasn't sad about having to drop out. She had very few talents. She couldn't sew, and she ruined everything she tried to cook, at first. She was afraid of the cows and chickens, but she helped me and Matthew gather eggs and milk the cow. What she did very well was cleaning and laundry. Our house and our clothes were spotless all the time. She and Benji had become close as well, but Benji loved everyone. That made it a little easier when it came time for me to go off to college a few years later.

Lorelei was judged by some of the church women, but most of them accepted her as they accepted our family. Papa faced down those that didn't and while they may not have liked her, they treated her with cool acceptance.

The sheriff did not arrest her father, but did talk to him.

There were a couple of occasions when he came to our yard in a drunken state and screamed obscenities and threats at her. It happened one time while Aaron was still at home. Aaron beat him with a board and bloodied him pretty good. Papa wasn't home at the time or I don't believe it would have happened. A few times after Aaron left for the army Lorelei's father came back and Papa was able to talk him off of the property. It seems he only beat helpless girls and backed down to men who stood up to him.

Lorelei was the middle of eight brothers and sisters. None of them ever came to visit her or Paul. It would have broken my heart if she hadn't had all of us to fall back on, but she did not dwell on it. She grieved more about the loss of Aaron, than the loss of her family. She came to love us as her family.

I went on reminiscing most of that Sunday. That night the nightmares returned. Fearful of falling asleep, I stayed up for the remainder of my time off.

CHAPTER 3
Breaking through

Monday morning before seven am, I reported back to Children's Hospital, glad to be back to work. As difficult as it was to be a woman in the medical field in the 1950s I was up to the challenge. Instead of getting discouraged, the skeptics and resisters spurred me on, and I was determined to win those folks over. Many children and mothers were much more accepting than fellow physicians. I was self-confident in this role.

Personal relationships were far more difficult. I had developed very few in college and in medical school. Older, experienced physicians advised and demonstrated treating nurses as subordinates that we must keep in their places. However, I learned early as an intern that experienced nurses could help me succeed or make life miserable. Still it was taboo to fraternize. Physicians had even more power to make life as an intern or resident miserable. I had developed no friendships among the doctors with whom I worked, not even Sarah Murdock, the other female resident.

I lived for my work and was empty away from work.

After receiving a report on each of the patients from Dr. Murdock, I began my seventy-two hours on-duty by making rounds with Nurse Cramer. The assignment included patients on the second floor, which was the post op floor, third floor-west, which was the medical floor, and fourth floor west, which was the polio iron lung unit. There were twenty-three patients in total, among them Willa, who was being cared for on the medical unit.

Her mother was not permitted to stay with Willa, but had to adhere to the same visiting hours as everyone else. I had spoken to the medical director on several occasions about changing the rules for visiting hours for mothers, but to no avail. Arguing that a mother's presence at the bedside would be beneficial to the child's recovery, I wrote a proposal for a research study on the theory. It was shot down without ceremony. Physicians and nurses did not want to deal with worried, sometimes hysterical parents twenty-four hours a day.

Willa was stable, medically. Her bleeding had not recurred. Her temperature and blood work were normal. Her face remained swollen and bruised. The left eye was sutured shut but blood-tinged drainage seeped out onto the dressing which had to be changed every few hours. Still there was no pus or foul smelling drainage to indicate infection.

Her mental state, on the other hand was fragile. She still wasn't speaking to anyone. When she wasn't sleeping, she was cowering and cringing whenever anyone approached her. When she received antibiotic injections three times a day, she cried. Her nightmares continued to awaken her and she would scream. She clung tightly to her mother whenever she was there. Although it was not protocol, the nurses allowed her mother to give her a bath, since she would not allow any of them to do it.

I sat down by her bed before attempting to touch her, and sat quietly for a few minutes without talking. At first, she would not look at me but after a while she peeped at me out of curiosity. I smiled and she dropped her head back down. "Its okay, Willa. You don't have to speak. Just shake your head, okay?" I said.

She shook her head, yes.

"My name is Dr. Rebecca. I was here when you came in. Do you remember me?"

She nodded her head yes.

"Do you hurt anywhere?" I asked.

Yes.

"Does your face hurt?" I did not ask specifically about her eye.

Yes.

"Does your head hurt?"

Yes.

"Does your belly hurt?"

Yes.

"And your arm?"

Yes.

"I am so sorry you're hurting," then I said to Cramer "Is she getting pain medication?"

Cramer looked at her chart. "She hasn't had anything today, doctor," Then she turned some pages in the chart. "I don't see where she has had anything," she said apologetically, her beautiful face pinched with concern. She was the Head Nurse and responsible for the actions of all the nurses on each shift. Some of the physicians would not address their young patient's pain unless they specifically complained of pain. The prevailing concern was that we might create an addiction in children. Neglecting the pain was a brutal practice, with which I would have nothing to do.

"Please bring her codeine right now, nurse," then to Willa "After that medicine is working, I will need to check under your bandage. May I do that? I will not hurt you."

She did not nod her head. I held out my hand and remained quiet. Again after a while of silence, Willa looked up. She saw my outstretched hand and cautiously reached for it, still holding her mother with the casted arm. Her body relaxed a little bit. I held her hand for a moment and waited for her to withdraw her hand first. She held mine for some time before bringing her hand back to her mother.

Cramer took me aside and whispered "You got farther than we have been able to, doctor. Maybe you'll be able to get through to her."

"She's in there, Sophie. She'll open up a little when she's ready."

Willa took the sweet red liquid medication. After it began to work she slept in her mother's lap for a while. I continued on my rounds.

Upon my return, Willa allowed me to check her eyeless socket and express a pocket of drainage. There was nothing suspicious of infection. I checked reflexes, and pupil response of the right eye, looked into her ears, and her throat. X-rays that first day had shown no fractures other than her arm and her face.

I needed to check for vaginal bleeding, but she had been repeatedly traumatized when some of the other physicians checked her against her will. Her mother was sent away each time, and she was held down. I would not do that.

Again I stopped and sat beside her bed. "I didn't hurt you, did I?" I asked her

No, she shook her head. Everything about her reminded me of Lorelei, not just her broken, casted arm. She was slender and petite. She attempted to hide her brutalized face in shame.

"I would like to check where you pee." She tensed up and held her breath momentarily. "I won't make you do it, Willa," I waited. "The doctors have told you that we had to sew up some cuts down there, right?" She did not nod or even look up. "I am worried about two things. One is that you could get an infection down there that could make you very, very sick. We are giving you antibiotics, hoping that you won't get an infection, but you still could if they are not the right antibiotics. The other thing I am concerned about is that you could bleed again. I know, Sweetheart, that it is uncomfortable; even embarrassing. If you let me check you, your mother can stay here. No one will hold you down. I will be very careful not to hurt you," I waited.

She got off of her mother's lap and crawled into bed. She also put her pillow over her face. I reassured her that only myself, Nurse Cramer, and her mother would be in the room. I warmed the speculum under warm running water, and was very gentle. Her stitches were still intact and there was no bleeding. When it was done, I praised her bravery and held her hand again. Then I let her know I would have to do the same thing the next day, but that she would have medicine for pain whenever she needed it.

She was left in the capable hands of the nurses as I went on with my rounds.

A short while later, Willa's mother wanted to talk to me while the child slept. We went in to a consultation room.

"I don't know what to do, doctor," she began to cry. "I cain't bring her back home. It isn't safe for her to be there. He won't leave her alone." It was then that I noticed a dark bruise to her left eye.

He, whoever he was, was attacking her as well.

"Did he do that to you?" I asked pointing to her black eye.

"I can take it. I been puttin' up with it for a long time. But I cain't protect my baby girl. I'm so ashamed. I lied about the bicycle."

I lowered my head, and looked at her under my brow and resisted crossing my arms to appear in judgment of her. Thinking carefully about my words I asked, "Have you told the police?"

"Yes. They wouldn't do nuthin' about it."

Dr. Fisher's irritation the first day was understandable. "Who is *he*?" I demanded.

"My husband. He's not Willa's daddy. I never married her daddy. Homer drinks. He gets mad and starts hitting me and the kids, but he started bothering Willa."

"How many children do you have?"

"Three. Willa's the oldest," she replied.

"Where are the other two? Are they safe?" I snapped at the woman. There had been no sign of other children. Were they still with her husband in harm's way?

"They have been staying downstairs here or with my neighbor. We haven't seen Homer since it happened."

"How long has he been raping her?" I asked boldly. She winced, and then cried again. Her full face was red with embarrassment, and wet with tears. She dabbed her nose with her soggy handkerchief, heavy with tears and snot.

"A couple of years, I think."

Rage roiled beneath the surface. It took a great deal of restraint for me not to throttle her. "So how exactly have you tried to protect her?" I didn't expect an answer. She would never be able to.

"The hospital will let the police know what you have told me. This is a crime. He WILL NOT do this again." The police had been notified by the nurse at the emergency room when the child came in, but there had been no follow up on their part.

"I stabbed him with a knife one time. I tried to kill him," Mrs. Lockhart asserted. "They put *me* in jail instead. Three times, I packed the kids up in the middle of the night, when he was drunk and ran away. He found us every time. I sent Willa 'way to Kentucky to stay with some friends. He found out where she was and sent a telegram to them that I was dead. They brought her back for my *funeral*. I have tried to protect her," she cried harder.

She did try to protect her children. My anger had been directed at the wrong person. Why didn't the police do anything? This time they wouldn't have a choice. If the hospital reported the attack, they would have to arrest this monster. I regretted the things I had thought and said. It was hard for me to accept that there was no one who could have stopped these attacks. I turned my rage toward God again. A loving God wouldn't let children suffer so.

CHAPTER 4
Sister Elaine Jayne, MSW

That afternoon I went to meet with Dr. Spence, the Medical Director, to speak to him about the discussion with Mrs. Lockhart. Dr. Spence was an aging fellow with a slight build, deep crow's feet at the corner of his eyes, a high forehead and an easy smile. He loved the children and took interest in each child; knowing them by name. They were more than *cases* to him. He could be tough with the physicians, nurses and staff when necessary, but mostly he was a good spirit, and a very approachable administrator. He was more like a father figure and did not evoke fear in me.

I knocked boldly on his office door. Instead of speaking an invitation through the door, he opened it and invited me in. His office was spacious with a wide, heavy cherry desk in front of a large window. Shelves lined the walls with an abundance of medical books, and anatomy charts decorated his walls. His medical degree and various certifications were framed and hung on the walls. Two upholstered chairs made of cherry sat in front of his cluttered desk.

"Good morning, Dr. Aldridge," he greeted me as he opened the door with a broad smile.

"Good morning, Dr. Spence. Do you have time that I might discuss Willa Lockhart with you?" I asked. He knew each child and their diagnosis. Involving himself in every case, he made rounds several times a day and spoke with each attending physician. He made time for residents, like me, as well.

"Of course, doctor. Have you seen her this morning? How is she doing?" he inquired with sincere interest. He motioned for me to sit in one of the chairs and he took his seat behind the desk.

We discussed my examination, assessment and observations, as well as the interaction with Willa. He posed some thoughtful questions to guide me further into her treatment, but refrained from telling me what I needed to do. I told him about the discussion I had just had with her mother.

He was equally appalled and in complete agreement with me that the police must be notified.

"This child and the others must be protected." He made it priority to notify the police of what we had been made aware. He also placed a call to Sister Elaine Jayne, a social worker from the diocese. I had never met Sister Elaine.

"She'll be able to help the child work through some of the emotional trauma she's experiencing. I've called her in before for children in need of assistance of various kinds. Nothing like this, but I am confident Sister Elaine will be able to help her and her mother," he explained.

Sister Elaine reported to the hospital within an hour of Dr. Spence's call. He called me into his office when she arrived. Sister Elaine, a petite young woman in her early to mid-twenties, stood no taller than my shoulders. She had delicate features with full pink cheeks. Her smile revealed small perfect teeth. She wore a simple gray dress and no veil, the uniform of the Sisters of Social Service.

Dr. Spence had given her only a brief account of what had happened to Willa. After introductions, I filled her in about the child, what had happened, and about the discussion with Mrs. Lockhart.

"Have you encountered a situation like this before, Sister?" I asked.

"I have not personally, but I think you would be surprised how often children are molested, doctor, or maybe you wouldn't. Have you seen many of these cases?" she asked.

"Not professionally," I answered, before giving much thought to the question. Why had I answered like that? I hoped neither she, nor Dr. Spence would seize the opportunity to pry into what I had just handed them. Graciously, neither one asked me personal questions, at least not then.

Sister Elaine followed me to the medical ward to see Willa and Mrs. Lockhart. She was very tender and gentle with both of them. Sister sat on the side of the bed near Willa and took her hand. The act of touch came as naturally to her as breathing. Mrs. Lockhart let Sister know right away that they were not Catholic. Sister assured them that being Catholic was not a requirement for her services, but Mrs. Lockhart remained suspicious. Willa seemed to almost instinctively trust her. She relaxed. She even spoke to her. Sister Elaine did not ask her about what had happened or what she was feeling. She stayed away from discussing the hospital, her family or her home.

"Have you been to the zoo?" she asked Willa.

"Yes," Willa answered through swollen lips.

They have a Panda bear. Do you think he looks like me?" Sister asked. Willa smiled through those swollen lips. "Maybe the monkeys. What do you think?" Sister added. Willa giggled. Then Sister asked her "What's your favorite animal?"

"Monkeys," she answered.

"If I could be an animal, I think I would like to be a giraffe. I would be able to see above crowds if my neck was that long. You see I am quite short. God has made some amazing creatures. Hasn't he?" she asked. Willa nodded. "What sort of animal would you be if you could?"

Willa thought for a moment, then said. "An Eagle." It is exactly what I would have expected. It is exactly what I would have answered.

"Why an eagle?" Sister asked.

Because I could fly away, I thought

"Because I could soar above everything," Willa answered. An eagle is everything she is not. It is strong and free with very few natural predators. It is not a victim. It is not ashamed. It is proud.

In my dream, I saw through the eyes of an eagle, flying higher than other birds could fly. Wind lifted my outstretched wings and far below I saw snow covered mountains and clear blue streams. Through eagles eyes, nothing was hidden. The longing to fly this way filled my soul.

A page to Dr. Spence's office once again interrupted my reverie. I excused myself and headed off to respond to the page. Two police officers stood in his office. Both were tall and fit with stiff military bearing. They wore their dark blue, sharply pressed uniforms with pride. Their request to interview Mrs. Lockhart and Willa worried me about how they might approach the child and make her relive the trauma. I expressed that concern to Dr. Spence and the police.

The one introduced to me as Officer Cooper, said "I understand ma'am. We will be as," he weighed his words carefully, "non-threatening as we can, but we still must investigate and for that we will need her testimony. What was done to this child was detestable; this man cannot get away with what he has done. We want to make sure we get all the facts and properly obtain statements and evidence so that when he goes to court he will be judged, and sentenced accordingly," he said "and doctor, we want her medical records stating her injuries."

I agreed and asked them if they could hold off just a while to question Willa. "The social worker is with her right now." I turned to Dr. Spence. "She is responding to her so well, Dr. Spence. This could be very therapeutic."

He agreed.

CHAPTER 5
The Connection

The first three hours Sister spent with Willa brought something out that was buried deep inside. For a moment she could forget her situation and be a child. When I heard Willa laugh for the first time, I suppressed the urge to cry. I hadn't cried for any of my little patients since I began my training; those emotions were excised in medical school. Pushing aside personal feelings and involvement is what made it possible to continue treating them even under the most heartbreaking situations, lest it render me paralyzed to do what was required.

Later while Willa slept, Sister spent an hour and a half with Mrs. Lockhart. Upon entering the room to let them know that she was awake, I saw Mrs. Lockhart crying and Sister hugging her. Sister was tending to the mother's recovery as well.

Sister made a difference. Day after day Willa improved physically and emotionally.

One Saturday afternoon, Mrs. Lockhart brought Willa's brother, Jerry, and sister, Joanie, to visit. They looked nothing like Willa with her fair freckled complexion, fine features and strawberry blonde hair. The younger siblings were olive skinned, brown eyed brunettes with coarse features, carrying themselves with defeated posture and worried faces. While Mrs. Lockhart denied that they had been abused to the extent that Willa had, yet it was clear that they had been physically and emotionally whipped.

Willa jumped out of bed at the site of them and ran to embrace them. Her arm still in a cast, she hugged them all the same. Joan cried and touched her face. She gently traced around her bandaged eye.

"I am so sorry, Willa," Jerry cried.

"Don't feel bad, Jerry. I'll be alright," she said.

"I'm sorry I didn't protect you," he sobbed.

Mrs. Lockhart and nurse Cramer cried at the sight of this little boy of eleven overcome with guilt because he couldn't stop the abuse. What a monster this man had been.

"Willa," her mother said, "The police arrested Homer, like they said they would. He's goin ta jail for a long time. 'm divorcin' him. He'll never bother us again."

Jerry, who had stopped crying was overcome with anger said "I wish he was dead."

Joanie on the other hand was torn "Daddy hurt us, Jerry, but he didn't kill anyone"

He had killed Willa's innocence, and maybe even her future. She might never be a mother. He had murdered her children to be.

Joanie continued, "Don't you remember when Daddy was nice? He played with us, and bought us presents, and took us places?"

"That was a long time ago. It's like that Daddy died, and this bad Daddy took his place," Jerry raised his voice at his little sister. Mrs. Lockhart shushed him.

Joanie began to cry.

Willa got very quiet and withdrew into herself as she

crawled back into her bed, pulled her knees to her chin and hugged her legs.

"I can see you are all very upset. Mrs. Lockhart, has Sister Elaine worked with Jerry and Joanie?" I asked as I stepped over and sat on the bed next to Willa. I put my arms around her as I had seen Sister do in the past.

"No. Do you think she would?" but before I could answer, she said to Willa "Oh, Willa, I almost forgot, Mrs. Hornsby, your old Sunday school teacher stopped by. She wants to come and see you."

I could feel the tension leave Willa's body at the mention of this woman's name. She looked up and pulled away from me excitedly.

"Mrs. Hornsby? Really? When?"

"She gave me her telephone number. I can call her tonight and see when she can come."

The children began to calm down and talk about going to Sunday school. It was the first time in a long time they had been to church, they explained to me. It was May and they looked forward to attending vacation bible school over the summer.

I began to reminisce about going to vacation bible school at my father's church every summer. What fun we had learning about Jesus, playing, and picnicking for a whole week. It was such wonderful fun each year until I was twelve-year-old, after that, I no longer enjoyed it. In fact, I resisted it but went because I was expected to go. It was my duty as the preacher's child.

Nurse Cramer invited Willa, her brother and sister to join the other children in the Day Room to watch our new television set. The *Uncle Al* show was about to start. Jerry and Joanie jumped with excitement, Joanie made little clapping motions with her hands. Bless Dr. and Mrs. Steinman who donated the new television set. It provided so much joy to the patients and their families.

A few days later I saw Sister Elaine in the hallway after a particularly difficult session with Willa. She could not discuss the content of her meeting with me but she assured me that Willa would be helped by the work they were doing. Sister said, "I will be available for Willa as long as I'm needed. That could be a very long time."

It was near the end of my shift and I was getting hungry. I happily accepted Sister's invitation to have lunch with her somewhere off hospital grounds. White Castle restaurant was only a short walk from the hospital. Neither of us had a car. My apartment was only a few blocks away from the hospital. Sister had the use of a car belonging to the Order when she needed one to see clients who lived further out, but since the House was within walking distance of the hospital she did not have need of it that day. She walked with a lighter step than I. It could have been that she was fresher than me. I had just come off another thirty-six hour on-call and had no sleep.

I remembered that Sister had told Willa she was quite short on the first day she had met her. She was indeed. She couldn't have been more than five feet tall. We must have looked the odd couple walking together. I was always self-conscious about my height, sprouting up in my early teens and didn't stop growing until I reached five foot eleven inches.

"Where are you from, Doctor? I detect a lovely southern drawl," she made small talk as we walked along the sidewalk.

"I was born and raised in North Carolina. My family is there."

"Where did you go to college?" she asked.

"I went to Ohio State University and Cincinnati University for medical school." I said anticipating her next question. "And you, Sister?"

"Why don't you just call me Elaine?" she invited. "I went to college in England, and did my post graduate work in

California. I joined the Order after college. They sent me on for a Master's degree in Social Work."

We found that we had a few things in common. My father and I had visited England and Ireland after I graduated from high school to visit my mother's extended family. Sister and I had spent time in some of the same places in England. We both loved children and had a passion for our work. But while we both had a strong connection to the churches in which we grew up, I severed my connection as far as I could and she sought to be more of a part of hers.

We also differed in our enthusiasm for food. When our food came, Elaine crossed herself and dived into her meal. She thoroughly enjoyed her hamburger and French fries. I ate because I was hungry but got little satisfaction from food. I had been that way for a long time.

After she finished her meal, she ordered a milkshake.

"We are expected to practice moderation in all things," she said apologetically. "But when it comes to eating, I lack discipline. Don't you like your hamburger?" she asked me.

"It's alright," I said.

"You must miss your delicious southern dishes," she offered in explanation for my lack of interest. In contrast to my indifference to food, she took great delight in drinking her milkshake.

I invited her to call me Becka, which is what my family called me. Since it was a public place we did not speak of Willa or any of the children, but kept the conversation light. We sat for a long time just talking. The restaurant was quiet in the late afternoon and we stayed quite a while. Being the only patrons, the waiter didn't seem to mind and came back frequently to refill my coffee cup. Before we knew it, the dinner rush started to arrive and we realized the lateness of the hour and concluded that it was time for us to go. We parted outside the restaurant and went opposite directions, me to my apartment, and her to the House.

Once again, in my little apartment, I wrestled with the reason I had no interest in food. It had nothing to do with missing "home cooking," it had everything to do with packing a picnic basket for Josh Stanford back in 1939. I remembered why I was so troubled about what happened to Willa. We had been connected by events in our lives.

CHAPTER 6

Amazing Grace

The day after Mrs. Lockhart told Willa that her Sunday school teacher wanted to visit, Willa was reunited with Mrs. Hornsby. The staff could barely wait to tell me about this enigma of a woman.

"She is beautiful. She looks like a movie star," one staff member said. "She dressed like a very wealthy woman. But not snobbish"

They all described her very differently;

"Rude"

"Sweet"

"Loud and flamboyant"

"Smart"

"Condescending"

It seemed that I had in mind the church ladies back home when first hearing about Mrs. Hornsby. In my day the church ladies were older, conservative housewives. They were homemakers, cooks and mothers. That seemed not to be the case with Mrs. Hornsby.

I couldn't wait to meet her since she seemed to intrigue

most of the staff but also because it made a difference in Willa. She was now talking to everyone. Her spirits had improved immeasurably.

Willa had been kept away from church for several years beginning when things changed at home. As the family's attendance became more sporadic Mrs. Hornsby called on the family only to be turned away by Mr. Lockhart. She wrote to Willa but the mail was intercepted.

Many aspects of Willa's life changed. School attendance was a problem. She wasn't allowed to play with her friends. He began to isolate the entire family from the outside world. Mrs. Hornsby shared her concerns and suspicions with the church's pastor, and the Elders. They tried also to contact Mrs. Lockhart and the children, but when she denied that there were problems and that they were looking for another church, it was then that the pastor and the Elders stopped trying.

I didn't have to wait long to meet the famous Mrs. Hornsby. She came to visit Willa every evening. She walked onto the area wearing a pale pink cashmere suit with a matching knee length sweater, white gloves and a pillbox hat. She had dark short styled hair and a creamy complexion with perfect make up. She was a very attractive, stylish forty something woman. She would not have blended in to a crowd, but instead command the center of attention by her very presence.

What could have attracted her to teaching Sunday school children? She would fit better into an adult cocktail party or opening night of a theatrical production.

I was documenting in a chart when Mrs. Hornsby stopped at the nurses' station. Her perfume, like fresh cut flowers reminded me of sitting on the porch of my father's house. She spoke to the nurse who was behind the desk preparing evening medications.

"How are you this evening, Miss Bell?" she asked in a sing-song voice.

"Very well, thank you, Mrs. Hornsby," Bell replied.

"How is my favorite patient doing this evening?" she asked.

"Looking forward to your visit. Willa is doing so much better since you started visiting."

"Well, then I shan't keep her waiting. I'm looking forward to seeing her as well," and off she went down the hall toward Willa's room.

"Bell?" I got her attention. "Is that the famous Mrs. Hornsby?"

"Yes. She is so nice. She stops and talks to all of the children and brings Willa with her. It's done Willa so much good," Bell replied

"I've seen the difference in her. But I didn't know she's been socializing with the other children," I said.

"She's made friends with Suzy and Macy. The three of them have been inseparable except when Sister is here. Willa wants time alone with her, but when Mrs. Hornsby is here Willa wants to share her with the others," Bell responded.

"Has Sister and Mrs. Hornsby met?" I asked

"They have, yes," Bell answered, and then quickly went back to pouring her six pm meds after noticing the Head Nurse, nurse Cramer coming down the hall.

I was left wondering how that meeting went, but Bell was obviously feeling watched as the head nurse walked passed throwing a stern glance her way.

"Dr. Aldridge," nurse Cramer acknowledged me. I returned the acknowledgment.

Instead of wondering, I decided to go and speak to Mrs. Hornsby.

The children's laughter and singing rang out through the hallway. They grew quiet as I approached, but the room was alive with excitement. All the children on the unit who could be out of bed were gathered around Mrs. Hornsby. Some children were in wheelchairs, others sat on mats on the floor and they were all smiling up at her. Willa sat in a chair next to Mrs. Hornsby and little Victor was on the lady's lap. She was reading from an oversized, beautifully illustrated children's' book. I had not seen the book before but the style looked familiar. She showed each picture to the children as she read the page.

Finally, I recognized the style. Mrs. Hornsby was reading a book by an author named Collette Genevieve, a well-known author and illustrator of children's books. I had watched several times during various story times when the nurses or volunteers read to the children, and this particular author was a favorite of the patients. I had long admired her books for the artful illustrations and uplifting message. They were simple enough for children to enjoy but profound enough for adults to ponder as well.

Mrs. Hornsby read a book titled *Popcorn Clouds* about encouragement and overcoming fear. I watched the expressions on the children's faces as they listened in wonder and anticipation. This woman could tell a story with great passion and expression. The faces of the adults listening mirrored the enthralled countenances of the children. Later, I learned that Mrs. Hornsby, herself, was the author and illustrator of these wonderful books and that Collette Genevieve was her *nom de plume*.

My attention to the story was interrupted by a page to Dr. Spence's office. Dr. Spence often kept late hours at the hospital. My meeting Mrs. Hornsby would have to wait.

"Have you had dinner, Dr. Aldridge?" he asked me when I got to his office.

"No, Sir. But I'm not hungry. I may have something a little later," I offered in explanation.

"Well, perhaps you'd accompany me down to the automat. I would like a little food. Maybe you would have a cup of coffee with me," he said kindly.

The invitation was unexpected as I had never received one before from him. Wishing not to appear rude I accepted, even though more pressing duties were waiting upstairs for me. But when the head of the hospital asks you to coffee you do not refuse.

Dr. Spence chatted merrily as we walked down the hall, got onto the elevator and rode down to the basement of the hospital. The halls in the basement were not as brightly lit as the other floors and a strong smell of bleach pierced my nostrils as I walked past the laundry department on the way to the automat. Dr. Spence kept the conversation light. At seven o'clock in the evening the cafeteria was closed and the only place to get anything to eat was in the automat. It was empty at this particular time.

"Is there something specific you wanted to discuss with me, Dr. Spence?" I asked directly. Sometimes I could be too direct.

"Oh, nothing specific, doctor. I would just like to know your plans after residency. Where do you see yourself in five years? Are you interested in remaining at Children's? Or do you intend to return to North Carolina to set up a practice?" he said as he made his selection of roast beef sandwich and a slice of blueberry pie. He put a dime into the coffee machine. "How do you take your coffee?" he smiled.

It sounded to me as if he were considering me for remaining on staff. I considered his first set of questions as I answered the last.

"Um, just—black, please," I stammered a little.

"Dr. Aldridge, may I ask you something personal?" he asked before I could answer his previous question about my plans.

"Of course," I said trying to sound self-assured.

"Do you have marriage in your future?" he was blunt.

I hesitated so he continued, "You are an attractive young

woman. And I am certain that medicine is your first priority, but is there a young man in your life?"

"There certainly is," I answered quickly. "In fact, there are several."

He drew his head back in surprise at my response.

"Victor Arcady, Tommy Brown, and Abe Williams to name a few," I named some of the patients and added seriously. "There are many, many more."

"Doctor…" he scolded.

"These are my life right now. I can't think of marriage and a family when all I want to do is see these children improve and have a future themselves. I did apply for the Bessimer Fellowship last month"

He smiled and handed me my coffee.

"I would love to remain here at Children's. In five years, I hope to have a pediatric practice, and I really hope it can be here in Cincinnati. As far as going home to North Carolina, I would be content to visit my father as often as I can but I don't want to move back there."

"Your residency is finished next month. Have you made plans in case you aren't asked to stay?" His words hit me hard. The time had gone so quickly. I had thought of some options, of course, but hoped to stay.

"Yes. Is there a chance you will offer me the Fellowship here?" It was my turn to be blunt.

"There is a very good chance, Dr. Aldridge. We've been very satisfied with your contributions to our hospital. I've received recommendation letters from Dr. Sabin, and Drs. Cliff and McKenzie. Things look good, but there are Dr. Roberts and Dr. Simms in the running as well," he said, sounding very serious.

It was a pleasant surprise to hear that Dr. Albert Sabin had recommended me. This was a real feather in my cap. It had been a stroke of luck that he had selected me from among many other applicants to assist in his research on the oral polio vaccine. Dr. Spence was cautioning me not to be too confident, but Dr. Sabin's letter carried more weight than any other.

"I was offered a position at Case Medical Center in Cleveland in their pediatric hospital. It's also an excellent hospital but it is my sincere hope to remain here. Dr. Sabin's vaccine is close to being released. Such exciting research in children's medicine is being done right here. It is a tremendous honor to be a part of it," my voice cracked with excitement.

"I would like to see the Fellowship awarded to you. So no marriage plans in the future?" he pushed the issue.

"No marriage plans. No. No relationships. Not even dating," I resented his prying a little. After all, certainly Roberts and Simms were not being asked these questions. They had no chance of getting pregnant, which, let's face it, was the real issue here.

For the moment this answer seemed to appease him. The topic changed to less serious issues such as baseball, astronomy, and bird sighting. He asked me about my thoughts about the idea of patient mother's rooming in with the patients. Did he really forget that I presented that to him or was he just testing me again? I repeated my original ideas and proposed that we do a research project on it. He admitted that he did remember that I at one time did write that same proposal. He said "I will bring it up with the board." That was further than I had gotten before.

Dramatic changes occurred in Willa's mood and behavior over the next several weeks. She was happy, extroverted and chatty.

"Good morning, Doctor Rebecca," she greeted me with a crooked smile. "How are you today?"

"Very well, thank you. I am happy to see you in such good spirits."

"Yes, I guess I am. I woke up happy today. I didn't

even mind another bowl of Cream of Wheat for breakfast. This is the thirty-sixth day I've had Cream of Wheat for breakfast. But you know what Dr. Rebecca? I'm not going to have Cream of Wheat forever. I'm getting better. One of these days I'm going to be able to eat pancakes and sausage again."

"Of course, you are. And it won't be long," I looked at her delicate face. The bruises had faded to a faint yellow now. Her missing eye had been replaced with a glass prosthetic. But I wondered what accounted for this about-face mood.

"Do you know why I woke up happy?" she asked, as if she was reading my thoughts.

"No. I really would like to know, though."

"Because I forgave him," she threw back her shoulders and raised her chin when she said it.

"Who?" I asked tentatively, fearing it was the monster who had done this to her.

"Homer," she said pertly. She used his name, instead of papa or daddy.

My heart sank. *Oh no*, I thought. *She's going into some psychological defense mechanism. This isn't good.* While she seemed good now, reality will come crashing back down on her.

I didn't want to be the one to do reality orientation and see her sink back into herself when we've worked so hard to encourage and promote psychological healing. It would do no harm right now if I just allowed her to talk.

"Have you read *Lovey the Lamb* that Mrs. Hornsby wrote?" she asked me

"No, I'm afraid I haven't," I said.

"It's good. She's a very good artist, too. She wrote it for children but it really is for everyone. Anyway, it's really about forgiving others. Do you know why Jesus wants us to forgive other people?" she asked.

I remembered the Sunday school lesson I had heard as a child, I said "So He will forgive us."

"Well, yes, that too. That's in the Lord's Prayer. 'Forgive our debts, as we forgive our debtors,'" she spoke so excitedly, "but he wants us to forgive people even if they don't deserve it. Because when we do that our own hearts start to heal. See when we hold hatred in our hearts that's all we think about. When I forgave Homer, I started feeling better. Even Cream of Wheat tasted good to me. Maybe that doesn't make sense but it's true."

"It makes a great deal of sense," I told her. Willa was remarkable and she inspired others around her. I continued to wonder if her revelation was wisdom beyond her years or a clever denial of the direction her life had taken.

She didn't sound delusional. She wasn't denying something had happened, but I wondered if this was a healthy reaction. Sister Elaine, later, admitted that she felt Willa's response was very healthy.

CHAPTER 7
The Monster

Elaine was becoming the friend I needed. At breakfast with Elaine the next morning, I was reminded about Willa's yearning for pancakes and resolved to make it happen the next day. Sister Elaine shared some of her cases with me and provided me with insight into Willa's reactions without betraying confidences.

"How can she forgive that monster?" I asked. "He is evil. What he did was horrible. I don't understand."

Her expression became soft with a slight knowing smile. She took a deep quiet breath before answering. "It's so much easier for a child with the right help than it is for an adult. But it's really the Holy Spirit that does the work of healing. You might reject this, being a doctor, but the real cure-giver is God. This type of injury is too deep for medicine to reach."

I didn't know how to respond, but it didn't offend me.

"Willa has been able to forgive so she can begin to move on. But her mother's pain is nearly unbearable," she said. I wondered if Mrs. Lockhart had told her about how I had judged her in the beginning; never even apologized for compounding her pain. I said nothing.

"Mrs. Lockhart needs a lot of help. She feels responsible for everything that happened to her children. She feels it's all her fault."

"But it's not," I objected.

"No, it isn't," Sister confirmed softly. I suspected that she knew how I had tried to blame her myself for what happened to Willa.

"We can't heal her pain by what we say, again that's the Holy Spirit, but many have made it worse by what's been said."

My eyes burned with tears. "I was one of them," I said.

"I know," she said without blame in her voice.

"It was how I asked her the question, not what I said, but *how* I said it."

"You weren't the only one. There were a lot of people," she said.

I said nothing.

"Most people get angry when a child is abused. Understandable. They feel helpless. We have to help Mrs. Lockhart with kind words, encouragement and support."

I interrupted her "An apology?" I asked.

"Would that help you?" she asked. Was that her way of admonishing me?

"I was wrong. I'd like her to know it," I was defensive.

"I meant, if you were in her place would an apology help you?"

Considering it for several moments I responded, "I don't know."

"She needs more. An apology is a start. If you can, you should follow through with help of any kind. Acts of kindness; on-going, when Willa is close to discharge. I'll be with the family for a long time, but if you can continue in any way you can, that would be good. They have to rebuild their lives. And we can pray," she said.

"I don't pray," I said. When she asked *Why not?* I just said "I will help the family after they leave the hospital, but I don't pray."

Sister didn't ask again.

We got to know each other a little better over time. She was fascinated that my father was a minister and even more fascinated that I no longer considered myself Christian. She tried to get to the reasons, and exactly when I separated from my prior faith beliefs, but I was vague and evasive. Sister never seemed to judge me or convince me that I was wrong.

"Do you doubt God's existence?" she once asked me.

"Oh, no. There is a God. I just have no use for Him," I responded quite nonchalantly.

But there was something Sister Elaine knew that I didn't.

"He'll be there when you are ready," she said.

She came to my apartment many times for tea when her schedule permitted. We always had a good time chatting, and laughing.

Her large family provided her with many stories. Sister was joyful and positive despite the type of work she was doing.

"Do you play cello?" she asked when she noticed the instrument sitting in the corner.

"Yes, but I try to be considerate of my neighbors. These apartments seem to have thin walls. I get to play once in a while when I'm home on a warm afternoon and windows are open and people are out. I've never had complaints but I don't want to bother anyone."

"Well, several of the Sisters play instruments. I, myself, play the clarinet. I think you might enjoy playing with us. What do you think?" she asked with a broad smile on her face.

"I would love that," I was excited about the idea.

Since my cello was too large to carry several blocks from

my apartment Sister was able to get the car to pick me up. There were thirteen Sisters living at the House. Elaine never referred to it as a convent. The House was in an old off campus dormitory that was once owned by the university. The dorm rooms used by the sisters as their "cells" were very tiny with smooth off-white subway style brick walls in the rooms and along a long corridor. There was a spacious kitchen and dining area as well as a Common Room. The Common Room was lined with bookshelves, hard wooden chairs and some end tables with lamps. It was used for gathering for prayer and scripture reading and singing. The musty smell of old books and burnt wood from the dormant fireplace was comforting to me; not unpleasant. Tall floor to ceiling windows were hidden behind heavy brocade drapes. This was a place where the Sisters could fellowship and sing and play their instruments. Nine of the Sisters played instruments. They loved to play music of all kinds although most of the music was religious or classical, but sometimes there was unexpected music like Dean Martin, or Bill Haley, Doris Day or even Elvis Presley. My favorite was *Unchained Melody* by Les Baxter. Some of the *girls* had pretty good singing voices as well.

These musical gatherings seemed to be very cathartic for all of us. Our "callings" as the Sisters called it were all very demanding and stressful. We would get together and play two or three times a month. I had longed for new friends; the Sisters slipped into my life to satisfy that longing. There was Sister Thomasina, who came from Africa, Sister Gertrude from Milwaukee, and Sister Laura from Chicago. There was a comfortable, familiar feeling with my new friends. Even when we shared meals and said grace, I felt more at home than uncomfortable about the blessing.

The last month of my residency went quickly, and I was planning a visit home when residency was completed. The Bessimer Fellowship was mine and I was to remain at

Cincinnati Children's. Willa was close to discharge at this time, and the family was doing much better as well.

The next ordeal was Homer Lockhart's trial. I was asked to testify to Willa's injuries and statements made by her and her mother on the night that she came to the emergency room. I was not anxious or nervous but I was angry. My anger over this didn't dissipate over the six weeks since it happened. The man was deplorable and his actions despicable. He had to go to prison for what he had done.

When Willa had told me she forgave him, I wanted to stir up in her the same anger I felt. But she had a greater grace than I. Sitting across the small table that served for mealtime she smiled knowingly at me. She told me that he had written her a letter and she wanted me to read it. Handing me the letter Willa said that forgiveness was up to her, because she knew that if Homer ever prayed to God He would forgive Homer. "So who am I to not forgive him, if God can forgive?"

The letter read:

> *Dear Willa,*
> *I have no right to ask for your forgiveness. So I am not asking. I cannot offer an excuse. There is no excuse for what I have done to you. You may not believe that I am sorry. But I am. When I married your mother, you were just a baby. I was the only father you ever knew. I know that I destroyed your idea of what a father is, too. You were precious to me then, and you are now. I don't want you to have to go through anything else about this awful thing and so I will plead guilty and do whatever it takes to spare you any more pain. If you can ever remember how our family was before I*

turned into this person I despise, please, think of those times.

Dad.

There was to be no trial. Homer pled guilty and was sentenced to twenty-five years in prison. She would not have to face "the monster."

"He was a Sergeant, you know?" Willa said. "During the war."

"No, I didn't know," I said. It didn't matter to me at that time.

"He was a hero. But he had nightmares. He never talked about the war, but I think he saw some terrible things when he was there. He didn't get drunk until he lost his job. We used to have a lot of fun when I was little," she said.

Willa's face was completely healed. Her beautiful blue eyes matched perfectly. She spoke often about "when I go back to school" and "when I go back to church" and her face would light up, but not as much as when she spoke about what Jesus had done for her.

Mrs. Lockhart had no forgiveness in her heart for her husband. Willa's little sister even had turned her pity for her father to doubt and fear. "I'm glad he's going to prison. I won't have to see him anymore," Joanie said.

"You said it before, Joanie, he wasn't always a bad man," Willa began pleading his case. "I remember when we went to the ocean on vacation. He taught us to swim in the ocean. He would throw us up in the air and we swam back to him for more. He helped you build a really big sand castle, too. Remember?"

"No. I remember him throwing you up against a wall," Joan scowled.

"Well, I remember a puppy for Christmas. Sammy licked him all over his face and he laughed and laughed. Don't you remember that, Joanie?"

"Yes," she said defiantly, "And I remember him dragging me by the hair outside, and I remember you screaming. I remember the bad things now more than the other things. Now, I'm not afraid when I come home. It's me and Jerry and Mama and soon you'll be home, too. And it'll be nice," she got quiet for a moment, then added "I have bad dreams about him hurting me like he used to hurt you."

So, I thought, *the family witnessed the whole thing.*

"Joanie, he's in jail now for a long, long time. He can't hurt you. Let's see you're eight-years-old now and he won't be out of jail for twenty-five years," Willa stopped and added in her head. "You will be thirty-three years old. We'll probably be married and have our own kids when he gets out of jail. You will probably never see him again."

It would be a miracle if Willa had children. I had long stopped believing in miracles.

Mrs. Lockhart tried to reassure her children, "As soon as we can afford it, we're going to move to another neighborhood, maybe another city. I have bad dreams too in that house."

Both girls said "No" at the same time. "I don't want to go to another church or school," Willa said.

"Me, neither," said Joanie.

"Maybe we could redecorate the house. Move things around and make it look different," Mrs. Lockhart said.

The girls agreed that it might make a difference.

Two short weeks later Willa was discharged. She had been there just short of two months.

CHAPTER 8

Confession

Nightmares haunted me on and off over the years. Since Willa was admitted the nightmares were unrelenting. One particularly disturbing dream was of being crushed under a large rock, I would wake up struggling to breath. In another dream, crowds of people, some of whom I knew and loved chased me and Papa from his church. The people were red-faced and angry, spewing hateful words toward us. Avoiding sleep, I stayed awake reading.

What had happened to me when I was her age was haunting me. On the outside I looked like a well-adjusted and successful woman, but inside I was anything but well-adjusted. It was difficult to develop close relationships since I left home and the ones I had from my youth were strained. I could not find forgiveness in my heart for the boy or even for myself. There were no visible scars like Willa's but there were definitely scars. The one man who loved me, George Anderson, I rejected because he deserved better than me.

Elaine kept gently encouraging me to open up to her. One

day I did, it was an evening that would begin my journey to healing.

She had been meeting me one evening a week for dinner at my place when we both were available. Spending time with my new friend made me feel giddy with excitement. I would spend the day sprucing up the apartment and cooking new dishes from whatever cookbook I found at the library. Sophie Cramer was able to join us at times making the evening merrier.

Sophie looked stylish in her street clothes. She looked forward to our "girl's night" as she put it. Sophie was slightly on the wild side and sometimes would bring a bottle of wine. Wearing slacks or shorts and drinking a glass of wine was about as *wild* as I would get. Having completed my residency meant that I had a little extra money to spend on myself. I bought some new fashions from the more expensive department stores even when they were not discounted or on sale. Wearing slacks was something I never felt free to do at home growing up. I felt rebellious and independent.

Elaine was never out of "uniform" wearing her gray nun's frock. It was not a full habit, but plain gray dress and apron with a white collar.

Cooking for my friends was a lot of fun. *Coq Au Van*, asparagus and croissant rolls was on the menu that night. Topics of discussion ranged from books we'd read, movies, television shows, the war in Korea and even politics. Occasionally religion came up, but I usually changed the topic when it headed that way. Sophie was quite funny with stories of her family. I would have loved to meet her mother from the things she talked about. Sophie could keep us laughing most of the evening when she started telling her tales of growing up in Cincinnati. If she spoke of the children at the hospital it was cute anecdotes or sweet stories. We never discussed the serious illnesses or injuries we saw daily. We needed to get away from all of that sadness. Sophie was a tough army nurse who had spent a tour in Korea before coming to Children's Hospital. She loved the children, but put on the self-protecting false front that she learned in the war.

After dinner we popped open the bottle of wine and adjourned to relax in the living room. As usual they offered to help with the cleanup, and as usual, I refused. The kitchen was very small and cramped, unlike the kitchen in Papa's house where a crowd could work together comfortably. The tiny apartment kitchen was efficient and organized and modern. The sink and appliances were pink and the walls were painted a mint green and white. A small white and chrome table with pink and green chairs was a comfortable arrangement for three women to share a meal.

My living room furniture was nothing fancy and after being invited to several of the doctors homes in recent days trying to impress the Bessimer Fellowship selection committee, I was ever more aware of how shabby my place looked. The boomerang shaped sofa was plain brown naugahyde with short stick legs, the two matching styles chairs were plain brown naugahyde and the trapezoidal coffee table and matching end tables also had stick legs. My interior decoration was stylish at the time for someone on a meager budget. These friends that I invited to dinner could graciously accept my modest apartment without judging. Having never been invited to the abodes of other residents, I had nothing with which to compare myself.

This night the topic of Willa came up. She had been home nearly two weeks, but Elaine was still working with her.

"Mrs. Hornsby is still helping the children. She has money, you know?" Elaine said as if it were gossip. "But she is somewhat of a philanthropist. Mrs. Hornsby has provided for Willa's tuition at a private school. She was having such a difficult time at the public school with children teasing her and she couldn't catch up with reading. Her loss of vision in one eye was a disadvantage in reading the blackboard," she sighed. "But she is blooming. She is so happy every time I see her."

"It's so hard to imagine what that child went through," Sophie said sadly. "Her childhood was stolen from her."

"Innocent lamb," Elaine added.

"Her innocence was stolen," I added bitterly.

"She is still innocent, Becka. She is still a child, too. With God's help she can enjoy childhood. Part of getting enjoyment in her life is the place she's gotten to – forgiveness," Elaine said.

Sophie's eyebrows raised and her lips pursed. Her emotions were easily read by her facial expressions. "He should be castrated!" she blurted out. "Did you read that bogus letter he wrote to her? He was just trying to look remorseful to get a lighter sentence."

"That may be," said Elaine "but only God knows his heart. And that letter did help Willa remember some good times."

Sophie, feeling the wine, started crying. "I ask all the time, how can God let children suffer like He does? During the war, the children suffered the most. Burns, land-mines, bullets – tore their little bodies apart. Stuff like this, what happened to Willa is intolerable," She cried. Elaine rubbed her shoulder while she cried.

When she regained her composure she spoke again. "Becka, I'm thinking I made a mistake going into pediatrics. I am reconsidering. Maybe I should go into either obstetrics, or maybe, take care of old people. When they die it's easier to deal with. They have lived their life to an inevitable end. Forgive me, ladies. I am sorry about this."

She got up and picked up her sweater, obviously, preparing to leave.

"Will you be alright Sophie?" I asked.

"I'll be fine. Please forgive me. I am so embarrassed," she sniffed.

"Sophie, there is nothing to forgive," I said "it gets to us all. Maybe you should stay and talk. There's no judgment here. I believe I've told Elaine that I have been angry with God for a long time."

Elaine smiled slightly, "No, you really haven't, but I knew you were. You chose to ignore that He exists but you told me that there is a God. So, I guessed that the distance between you and God was your anger."

"No. No. No," Sophie objected "I'm not angry at God. That would be a sin. I just don't understand Him"

"Is anger at God a sin?" Elaine asked. "I'm not so sure about that."

"Of course it is," Sophie sounded shocked at the suggestion coming from a nun.

"Have you ever been angry at someone you love?" Elaine asked in her gentle tone.

"Yes, but that's different. I've gotten angry at my mother many times, James, too." James was one of her brothers. This was another family member of Sophie's I would have liked to meet, too.

"Did you hate them?" Elaine asked a leading question.

"No, I was angry but I didn't hate them. But they aren't the Creator of the universe."

"The God of the universe will forgive anger, even at Him. In fact, Jesus was angry. He was so angry that he overthrew tables in the temple. There is nothing fair, no good thing conceivable about these things that you are talking about. While I would never say this to the child or the families I counsel, because it would sound trite, but God is in control. The devil causes all this evil in the world, but God will use it for good. We may not be able to see the big picture, but God is good. He does not cause any of this.

"Maybe Willa's trials will lead her or someone else to do a lot of good for others. Her forgiveness of her attacker," Elaine did not call him her father or the monster "may lead him to a reformed life, even in prison. We may never see the good God will bring out of this but He will bring good. The thing is each of us; our life here on this earth touches others, either for good or for bad.

"There is something about your experience in Korea that led you to pediatrics here. You do good every day, Sophie. Becka said it. This is a safe place to talk. We are friends. There is no judgment."

"That's all there is to it, girls. I saw a lot of horrors over there, and I guess I am angry at God. I guess the sin is that I know it and I'm not ready to ask forgiveness. I'm guessing you heard all the grotesque details of what happened to Willa, Sister. How do you deal with it?" Sophie asked.

"Prayer. A lot of prayer," she answered.

"Well, ladies, I think the discussion has gotten very serious. I would rather listen to some music," I said to change the subject.

"Do you dance?" Sophie asked. "I love to dance."

"So do I," said Elaine to the surprise of both of us.

"Well, doctor, what have you got to dance to?" Sophie asked heading toward my record cabinet. She selected Fats Domino and placed the vinyl disc on the suitcase record player. I was feeling the wine, too. We danced and laughed and I forgot about my neighbors, and if they would be disturbed.

By eleven o'clock we were all exhilarated and exhausted. Elaine had forgotten that she had a curfew and had to leave. Sophie admitted that she had to work early the next day, so both got ready to leave.

Sophie left first, and even though Elaine had a curfew, which she had already missed, she lagged behind. She wanted to talk to me; or rather she wanted me to talk to her.

"So, Becka, tell me. It's time," Elaine said.

"Tell you what?" but I knew what she meant.

"When I first met you, I asked you if you had seen cases like Willa's. Do you remember what you said?" she walked over to the couch and sat down. I sat beside her.

I remembered, but I said "That was a long time ago."

"You said 'not professionally,' which I'm guessing meant that you had personal experience."

"I can't talk about this, Elaine. I've buried it so deep that it doesn't hurt anymore. In fact, I don't feel anything. And I like it that way," I sounded more defiant than I intended.

In her best counselor manner she carefully considered her response. She looked me in the eye and took both of my hands in hers. "You don't feel anything?" she repeated gently.

I looked back into her eyes, agitation churning. I repeated "And I like it that way."

She was silent for a long time. I looked down. I knew that looking someone in the eye said *I'm confident; I'm honest; I'm not afraid*; but I could not maintain eye contact. Through all the challenges of being a female in the male dominated world of medicine, I had long forced myself to look people in the eye, but was never confident or unafraid.

After my gaze had fallen to our hands, my shoulders slumped and out of some place buried deep inside I began to sob. What a liar I was.

She gently touched my shoulder with one hand as I cried.

Finally getting control of myself, I apologized profusely. "I don't know where that came from. I have never done that before."

Elaine had tears in her eyes as well. "Oh, my dear friend, do you know what Jesus did when he heard that his friend Lazarus had died?"

I remembered that, "He cried," I answered.

"It is the shortest verse in the Bible. ' Jesus wept.' He not merely cried but he wept. It seemed to me odd when I first heard that story. Jesus knew that He could raise Lazarus from the dead, so why did He weep?" She paused with tears in her own eyes.

I didn't have an answer.

"I think it was because His heart broke for those around Him. Lazarus' sisters and friends were despairing over his death. Jesus was human and He felt their anguish. Humans feel, Becka. We feel."

"No," I protested "I don't want to feel the pain. It's too much."

"Numbness can't last a lifetime. That pain that you buried will seep out in other ways. None of them healthy," Mercifully she didn't list what she had observed in me. "You don't have to tell me. Not ever. I love you and none of us is undamaged. But, just know I'll be here for you if you are ever ready to face that pain. You won't have to face it alone."

I briefly wondered what damage had happened to Elaine. She embodied joy. Many times I found myself wishing that I had what she had.

But my thoughts returned to myself. I looked into her lovely face, and told her what I had never told anyone before "I was raped when I was twelve years old." She didn't look shocked. She didn't look disapproving. So I continued, "Willa's age, but he didn't beat me or hurt me like she's been hurt."

"You don't need to minimize what happened to you by comparing it to what happened to Willa. The injury to you has impacted your life all this time," she said.

I continued, "There was a boy, a lot older than me. He was sixteen and all the girls had a crush on him; even me. He was a very good baseball player and everyone in the county thought he was a big deal. He was like a movie star. They all thought he would be a big league baseball player someday. And he is, actually.

"It was Independence Day and we were having a big festival in the town. All the churches had one big picnic. There were games, and booths, and a beauty pageant, and of course a baseball game.

"I was very shy, and a daddy's girl. I had on a new blue flocked dress with ribbons my aunt had made for me and the same ribbons in my hair. I thought I was – I don't know, a princess or something. One of the ladies sent me to fetch some ice at the ice house.

"Nobody was around and Josh came up to me. Josh was the boy. He asked me for some ice, but he also flirted with me. I was so flattered that he was even speaking to me. When he told me he had noticed me watching him play ball and that he knew who I was, I was so excited. He knew that I was the 'preacher's kid,' That's what he called me.

"I asked him if he would like to come to our church's table for the picnic. He said no. But, he told me, if I wanted to bring some food to him after the ballgame he would like that. He told me to bring it to him and that he would be on the footpath in the woods.

"He never told me not to tell anyone, but for some reason I didn't. Not even my best friend, Heidi. She had a bigger crush on him than I did and I was afraid her feelings might be hurt if he paid attention to me and not to her.

"Papa had brought a little picnic basket from home with some butter and jam in it. I took that one and packed it full of fried chicken and corn on the cob, and green beans and cherry pie that the other ladies had made. But, I told no one that I was doing it. I was thrilled along with everyone else as we watched Josh pitch a no-hitter and his team won. My brother Aaron played against him. Aaron was pretty good, too, but no one was as good as Josh.

"So a little while after the game and all the adulation for Josh died down he was able to walk off. I watched him go down the footpath and no one followed him. When I went down the path there were a few pairs of lovers walking back to the picnic. The path forked and I didn't know which way to go, then I heard him whisper from the brush. He thanked me for the picnic basket and grabbed my hand and walked down the path. He walked very quickly and was pulling me pretty far into the woods. I couldn't hear the noises from the festival by the time he stopped.

"He started kissing me. But it scared me. It wasn't like I had seen in the movies, you know, soft and romantic. It was rough and I was frightened. I tried to push him away, but then he pinned me down and ripped off my – my panties. He hurt me," again I cried. I had told her before that he had raped me but couldn't say the word now. I felt guilty that I had been so excited over his attention, that I practically skipped down that path with a picnic basket in my hand.

"Afterward, he sat back and ate the food I had brought him. He even offered me some. I was angry at him and knocked it out of his hand but he laughed. I asked him why he had done it. He told me it was my fault. He said that I was flirting with him, teasing him. That's when he said that if I told anyone, that people would believe that I had *asked for it* and that people would believe him. He said 'people love me' who did I think they would believe? He told me that my father might be kicked out of his church for raising such a bad girl.

"Elaine, that wasn't the only time he did it either. He told me that if I didn't meet him again, he would tell people. I believed it." I told her everything.

Elaine finally spoke, "So no one ever found out?"

"I couldn't tell anyone. I believed him that my father would lose his church. I guess I believed him that I was a bad girl. I think Aaron might have figured something out. He asked me questions about why I didn't want to go anywhere, or do anything. He specifically asked me if anyone was bothering me and started walking me home from school every day. That was when Josh stopped."

"Who's Aaron?" Elaine asked.

"He was my oldest bother."

"Was?"

"He was killed in action during the War," I said

Elaine dropped her head for a moment, and then looked back at me. Her mouth softened into a sad understanding smile. "Do you still believe the things Josh said?"

This was another thing I had not given any thought. "I don't know."

"Well, I know. He was a liar. He was the one who knew what he was doing was wrong. You are not to blame for what he did to you," she placed emphasis on he. "That's the first thing we have to work on, Becka. Forgive yourself. You did nothing wrong. You can be angry with God but God didn't to this. There is evil in this broken world. Homer did despicable things to Willa. This Josh did despicable things to you. And both of them are human beings, not the devil, himself. Both of them have mothers and fathers and probably at least someone who loved them. The hardest thing to accept is that God loves them, too. And that Jesus died for them just like He died for our salvation. When you can forgive this boy you can move on, but Becka, I think you'll need to start by forgiving yourself," she paused.

"I don't know how to do that, Elaine." At least I had stopped crying. I began thinking she could help me finally work through this. "But — you just told me I am not to blame. Why do I need to forgive myself?"

"You aren't to blame, but I don't think you believe that," she said kindly.

Elaine sat beside me and held me in her arms and let me cry until I couldn't cry anymore. She stayed with me, sitting quietly until I fell asleep. She went home sometime during the night after I fell asleep. Later, when I woke up still laying on my sofa, I felt like a weight had been lifted from me. I was even hungry.

Before she left, Elaine had straightened up my apartment, put away the record albums, and washed and put away the dishes.

The oatmeal I had made for breakfast, embellished with brown sugar and raisins was so good I had a second bowl.

CHAPTER 9

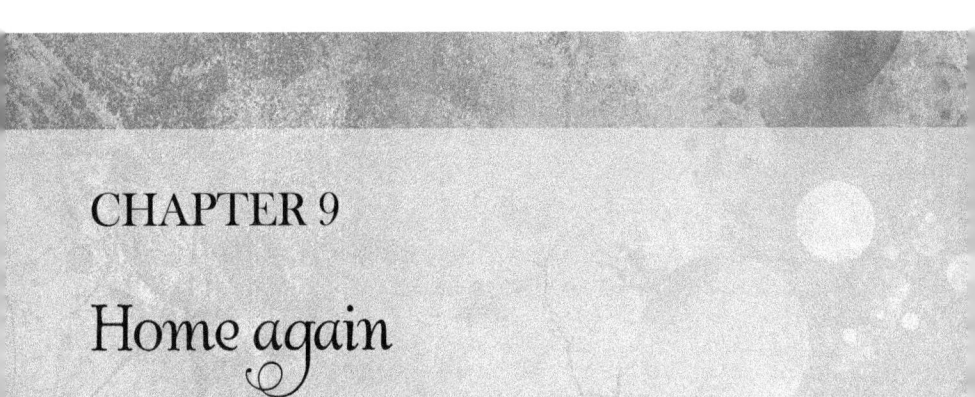

Home again

June 1956

The hospital gave me two weeks off before beginning work as a full time attending physician. I travelled back home to spend that time with my father and the family. There was an empty feeling every time I came home for a visit now since Benji had passed away a few years before. He had lived longer than expected for someone in his condition. My brother Matt and his family planned to join us for a family reunion.

This trip though gave me time to think about things. I bought a car which meant no bus or train travel this time. It was a darling light blue Ford Thunderbird with a removable fiberglass top and white vinyl seats. The car was a year old but absolutely beautiful. I secretly enjoyed one-upping my brother Matthew. He loved to show off how much money he was making as a banker by buying conspicuous cars and clothes.

Since I didn't know what to expect with the weather the top was left on for the trip because if it had begun to rain I would not be able to lift the top back on by myself. The trip took six hours through the Interstate 21's twisting windy roads but the weather was gorgeous. The views were so lovely that several times I just parked along the roadside and looked over the mountains in West Virginia. God's creation comes into focus when looking at the beauty of the mountains. Elaine was right; I couldn't deny that God existed.

The long drive home gave me a lot of time to think about Willa and Josh Stanford. I also thought about God and how could He allow these things to happen. Elaine's words echoed in my thoughts "God didn't do this but He will use it for good."

But how could that be? From the moment it had happened to me I had been changed. The care-free child had evolved into a guilt-ridden, terrified person, afraid that everyone would find out the terrible thing I had done. I felt vile and undeserving of anything good in my life.

As I drove, it dawned on me, that I had not only been angry with God but angry with Papa too. None of that made any sense, of course, Papa wasn't to blame. However, in my childhood world Papa was a man of God. He was God's representative. If God knows all things and did not stop it, why didn't Papa know and protect me? Maybe I had been unlovable all along.

Aaron had noticed the change in me that Papa had not, but Aaron could not get me to talk about it. I became withdrawn. Even Heidi and her mother commented on the change in me.

"It's like you're living under a dark cloud, child. I hope you snap out of it soon," Mrs. Anderson said. She told Heidi that she thought I was feeling left out of the things that daughters did with their mothers and so she tried all the harder to make me feel like I was one of her own.

Still, I could never be 'good enough,' so I worked harder

and studied harder to prove myself worthy. Nothing, however, absolved me of that guilt.

Papa never failed to tell me how proud he was of me with all my accomplishments. He praised all of us, Aaron, Matthew, me and Benji. He encouraged us, and he gave each of us his time. He had Bible study and prayer time with us every morning. He read us stories and listened to us read. He took us to picture shows, listened to the radio, took us swimming, hiking, horseback riding, and to fairs and carnivals. He took Aaron and Matthew camping at least once a year. Papa spent more time with us than any of my friends fathers spent with them.

None of that changed how I felt. I never even realized that I was angry at him until recently. So during the drive home I resolved to tell him what happened when I was twelve and ask him for counsel so I could heal and mend relationships, just as Willa had begun to heal. I rehearsed many conversations in my head as I drove, but I was scared, unsure of how he might respond.

Since I started out at one o'clock on the afternoon, the plan was to drive straight through and get there after dinner time if weather and traffic allowed and that I would stop and have dinner before getting home to Belmont. It felt strange turning down the road leading home driving my own car. Papa had always picked me up at the train station or bus station before this trip. It was he who drove down the street each time I returned home.

I drove past Papa's church. The sign by the road read Living Water Church; Jesse E. Aldridge, Pastor. It was a large, old, stately church that had been added on to as membership grew over the years. It was a brick building with a flat roof and a belfry with a steeple and a cross on top. Something drew me to turn the car around and go back to the church. The driveway went right up to the front doors which allowed folks to drop off church goers who were weak or elderly. I pulled my car around to the side entrance which was near my father's office. This was the way I customarily went in. I got out of my car and walked up the three steps to a landing by the door, but the door was locked, so I drove around to the back door of the church. The entrance to the social hall was unlocked.

It was not surprising to find the church unlocked. Papa and the trustees agreed that the doors would be open each day until nine pm, whether he or a trustee was there or not. It was to encourage a soul in need to seek God in His house. Then each night someone was scheduled to come and lock the doors. Maybe, I was the soul in need to seek God this day.

The bright sunshine came at an angle through the windows in the social hall, gleaming off of the tile floors. There were long rectangular tables set up with chairs at each one. The kitchen had been updated the year before and was full of large gleaming stoves, refrigerators, deep stainless steel sinks and counters to prepare large meals for congregational dinners, funeral dinners, weddings and such. A walk up the stairs led to a hallway. The hallway leading to the sanctuary had four doors to Sunday school classrooms along both sides. I opened the heavy cherry wood door at the other end of the hallway, entered sanctuary and stepped into the past. Rows of white painted pews faced the chancel area in front where the pulpit and choir stands stood. The familiar old pipe organ stood off to the right as I walked in and a new upright piano was placed beside it. Papa had been pastor to a smaller church when I was young, before coming to Living Water Church. The other church was stuffy, full of stiff necked people; often judgmental and sometimes cruel in what they would say. Even the old church building itself was dark and unwelcoming. When we came to Living Water Church we felt at home and loved as a family. I was seven years old and Mother had already died. Heidi became my best friend on that first Sunday in church. I thought of Heidi as I walked past the Sunday school doors and pictured the two of us fidgeting and laughing during church service and her mother tapping us on top of the head and shushing us, pinching our thighs or making us change seats and sit on either side of her, if we didn't take the first warning.

Every week, Heidi, Matt, George, Aaron and I would stand up behind the pulpit with the rest of the children's choir and sing with all our hearts to please the Lord, proudly wearing our choir robes.

Heidi, now married with a little boy, still attended this church every Sunday along with her husband, her mother and father, and her grandmother.

I walked over and sat in the pew alone for a few minutes. Nothing came to mind to pray. Then I thought of Elaine's words to Sophie. "The God of the universe will forgive anger, even anger at Him"

God, it's been a long time since I even wanted to talk to you. I know I need your help. But I am so angry at You. It is hard to ask for help from someone that you are angry at. Maybe that's where I need to start. Can you help me stop being angry? I prayed without speaking out loud. I thought of how empty I felt. I had been trying to fill the emptiness with hard work, money, new clothes and a new car. These things weren't doing the trick. I continued praying; *Of course, I am angry at Josh, too. I guess I have been angry with myself as well. How can I forgive if my mind is so clouded with anger? Am I too self-absorbed? I try to think of others and not of myself but Lord I don't know what I'm feeling. I don't want to hurt anymore, God. Help me to stop hurting.*

I sat quietly without praying, both physical and mental pain began seizing my body and mind. I cried, again. How I hated crying! Was this the answer God was giving to me?

When I finally left the sanctuary, after everything subsided, I felt hollow.

Walking down the hallway, away from the sanctuary, I heard distant voices coming from downstairs in the Social Hall; there were others in the church that had not been there when I entered. I ducked into the small bathroom between the class rooms to check my face. No red splotches betraying what I had been doing; my black hair remained contained in its tight twist behind my neck; and after touching up my lipstick, it was clear to approach whoever belonged to the voices. The closer I got to the social hall, the more discernable the voices became. There were children's voices, as well as some women talking and another singing happily.

Two preschool age children played in the Social Hall. One was Mitch, Heidi's four year old son. The other child was about the same age but I did not recognize him. Mitch did not recognize me, but that was understandable. He hadn't seen me for about a year and that was only in church one Sunday.

Of course, Heidi was close by, looking very pregnant. Heidi was standing on a ladder trying to help another woman hang a banner made from butcher paper. The words caught my eye:

Happy Birthday, Becka

They had been caught in the act. My birthday was the next day and they were preparing a birthday party for me. I was not sure who the woman on the other ladder was, but she did look familiar.

It wasn't until Mitch, who suddenly shouted "Hi. What's your name?" as he walked over to me, that the women looked over at me.

"Becka!" Heidi squealed in a mixture of excitement and disappointment. "What ah you doing heya?"

She got clumsily down from the ladder allowing her end of the banner fall to the floor. Her partner was left holding up her end.

"What are you doing on a ladder in your condition?" I responded.

Heidi ran to me and threw her arms around me. Mitch ran over and wrapped his arms around my leg.

Before Heidi could say another word her mother, the woman I had heard singing in the kitchen, yelled "Rebecca Allison Aldridge, you ah NOT sposed to be heya," she was clearly upset. Mitch jumped back and looked over at her.

"I'm sorry, Mrs. Anderson. I didn't know. Can I pretend I never saw anything?" I asked.

Heidi laughed "Ah don't think so. Ya'll can't keep a secret very well."

Except the biggest secret in my life that I kept from everyone for the past fourteen years, I thought.

Mrs. Anderson walked over to me to offer a hug as well. She had been slowed to a snail's pace with the advance of her arthritis. The image of her dancing in her kitchen with us when we were children flashed in my memory. She treated me like one of her own back then, but when I broke her son, George's heart, the relationship between Mrs. Anderson and I changed, but she always remained kind, and gracious toward me.

"Hello, Becka. Welcome home," the other woman said as she rolled up the banner. I finally recognized her.

"Wilma Fauntleroy. How have you been?" I asked.

"Fine," she said in her delicate southern drawl, "this youngin keeps me hopin' tho," she looked at her son who was running around the room pulling a toy dog on a rope. I recalled his name was Roy.

"Hello, Roy," I said. My greeting fell on deaf ears. He was engrossed in leading his little toy dog across the shiny floor.

Wilma walked over to me and hugged me. Most people in our church were huggers.

Heidi said. "You wah sposed to go home fust and they wah sposed to keep ya busy til tamarra."

"Well, I was driving by and had the inexplicable urge to come into the church. So, I did," I smiled.

"The s'prise is spoilt. I hope yah not disappointed!" Mrs. Anderson said,

Before I could answer she went on "We ah so glad to see ya. How's it been goin up theya in Ohio? Yah beginnin ta sound like a Yankee more and more ever tahm I see ya," her disappointment had dissipated.

"By the time I go back, I'll sound just like ya'll," I said. Then to Heidi, "Your due date is coming up soon, right?"

"Three weeks. July twelfth," she smiled

"That's fah weeks, Shug,"Mrs. Anderson corrected her.

"Three and a half weeks, but I'm gunna go early," she said.

An excited voice came from the door "Whose cah is that out theya?" It was my nephew, Paul.

This time it was me who squealed "Paul, baby. How are you?" as I ran to hug his neck. He let me hug him which is never easy for a fourteen year old boy. He looked so much like Aaron that my heart broke each time I saw him. I was so very proud of my nephew. Paul was a strong, smart and kind young man.

"Ah'm doin' fine, Aunt Becka. How ah you?"

"Great now. You've grown a foot since last year," I gushed

"Naw. Maybe a little taller. Really, is that yah car?" he asked again.

"Do you like it?" I asked.

"Ah, Lawd. Do ah like it? When kin ah drive it?" he was so excited he could barely contain himself.

"Now, if you like. You can drive us home," I said. His expression was priceless but before he could answer Mrs. Anderson interrupted.

"Paul, what did you come for? Did you need something?" Mrs. Anderson asked.

"Oh, yeah. Well, never mind," I knew he didn't want to be the one to spoil the surprise.

"T's all right, Paul. Becka knows. She saw the sign," Heidi laughed.

"Ya did?" he said, a little disappointed.

"I offered to pretend that I didn't. Heidi just laughed at me. So you can say whatever it is that you need," I said.

"Mama just wanted to know what time for sure we're sposed to bring Aunt Becka tamarra."

"We'll be ready 'bout one o'clock. But don't tell Becka," Mrs. Anderson said. "we don't wan ta spoil the s'prise."

Paul looked confused, but his eyes light up when I handed him my car keys. I said good bye to my friends and let Paul drive me home, after he helped me take the removable top off and put it in the trunk.

Papa did not live in a parsonage anymore, so he was not answerable to trustees when it came to our home. He had purchased a house within walking distance of the church just two years after we moved to Belmont. Papa had means after his Uncle Samuel left his entire estate to his only living relative. He did not spend money frivolously but he put me and Matthew through college and me through medical school; just as Uncle Samuel sent him through college. Papa was going to send his grandsons and granddaughters through college as well.

I loved pulling up the driveway to that big wrap around front porch with a swing, and rocking chairs and even a table and chairs. Two large Magnolia trees were in bloom, the heirloom yellow tea roses climbed the right porch pillar and trellis beside it. There were two old peach colored Floribunda rose bushes on each side of the front steps. Behind that was a large lilac bush that had bloomed earlier in the spring. The floral smells were intoxicating. A garden path drifted off to the right side of the porch passing under an arched garden gate. As I looked at the front of my father's home memories flooded back of family and friends playing music and just loving on each other on that porch.

Lorelei ran out of the house to greet me. She hugged me quickly and stepped aside as Papa stood patiently behind her, waiting his turn. He still looked handsome to me, even at sixty-nine years old. Papa was six foot five inches and still stood tall and muscular with large strong hands. His wavy hair was silver now.

And he was still strong. He picked me up off my feet when he hugged me. Papa smelled like witch hazel and fresh cotton. I nuzzled my nose into his neck, and heard him laugh. "Welcome home, baby girl," he said.

"Ah ya hungry?" Lorelei asked.

I had eaten just a few hours before so that she wouldn't have to cook for me, but she had. I had told them my plan to stop somewhere for dinner before coming home. She had learned to cook and was very good at it now. I shouldn't have taken that, her gift to me, away from her. How could I eat again?

"Did you make dinner?" I asked. It was nearly seven o'clock. I had hoped they had not waited for me.

"You know she did," Papa said. "I reminded her that you were going to stop before you got here. You did stop and eat right?"

"I did. Hope ya'll didn't wait for me," I said.

Lorelei didn't sound disappointed when she said, "It's alright sweetheart. We ate a few hours ago. I just thought you might want some tea and a cake."

"We didn't have dessert," Paul added. "Coconut cake. Can't wait."

I heard a bleating sound from around the back of the

house, along with the usual clucking of chickens. "Papa, what am I hearing back there?"

"After Moo died, I got some goats for milk. We got babies. Do you want to see 'em?"

He led me around to the back of the house to the small barn that used to house the cow. There were four goats; two kids and two grown brown goats. Chickens pecked their way around the barnyard off to the back corner of the yard, away from the flower garden. The barn had a new coat of red paint. A fence separated the animals from the vegetable garden and the flower garden. The kids were adorable. They came up to me to be petted.

"Did you name them?" I asked him.

"Jack and Millie are the parents. I'm not keeping the kids, so I call em *For Sale* and *Barter*," he teased.

"Well then I think I'll call them Sal and Bart," I returned the banter. "You've got a new flock." He always referred to the congregation as his flock.

We went into the house and I forced myself to eat a piece of Lorelei's coconut cake and some tea. Although I was exhausted from driving all those hours, I didn't want to let this time go. We stayed up until after midnight just talking and laughing.

CHAPTER 10
Family and Friends

I squinted at the bright sunlight, softened by the sheer ruffled curtain, to focus my eyes. The delicate white curtains billowed gently by a breeze blowing through the open window. Sleeping in my old room was sublime. My sleep had been dreamless and restful.

Lorelei knocked lightly on my bedroom door. "Becka, honey, ah ya ahwake?"

"I am. I'll be down in a couple of minutes," I hadn't been awake but it seemed lazy to be sleeping when others were up at the crack of dawn. Residency meant keeping unusual hours but I had also gotten used to waking up quickly; ready to function on little sleep. It was already ten o'clock. *Breakfast?* Were they all waiting on me?

Now, in my father's house we did not come down to breakfast in our night clothes. The minister expected to have people unannounced show up at our door at any time with an invitation into our home. Anyone could be sitting in the kitchen when we came down. So, even in the middle of the night, we got dressed to come downstairs even if it was just to use the toilet. I dressed in slacks and a breezy cotton blouse dotted with tiny blue embroidered flowers. Papa had never expressed an opinion about women in pants but it was a pretty rare occurrence in my home town in those days.

This morning the kitchen was filled with activity. Matthew, his wife, Ginny, and their three children had arrived from Raleigh early. I had slept through whatever commotion they had made settling into their room down the hall.

Dr. and Mrs. Stanton were sitting at the kitchen table having coffee with Papa. June Russell, a woman from church, was helping Lorelei.

"Welcome home, Dr. Aldridge," Dr. Stanton was the first to greet me. He got up from his chair and came to give me a hug. He had called me Becka up until the day that I received my medical degree and then it was nothing but 'Dr. Aldridge' as a sign of respect.

"Good morning, Dr. Stanton. Mrs. Stanton," I gave her a hug. She was one of the sweetest women I had ever known; always kind and positive. I imagine that she had never had an unkind thought about anyone. And she had loved Benji so.

Afterward I was greeted and hugged by everyone else in the kitchen.

Matthew was even taller than Papa but thinner. Like me, maybe he was considered underweight. But Ginny made up for both of us. She was rather stout and short. It reminded me of the children's poem about the little teapot every time I saw her. Her cheeks were rosy and her fine blond hair gathered in a bun with little wisps flying free. She had an endearing British accent that charmed the people in our church. Matt had met her in England when he went abroad to study. They argued in public on occasion but mostly seemed to make up and get along very well.

Matthew had a way of calling her "woman" that just irritated me. I had told him so several times. The way he said it made him sound as though he thought men were superior to women in general. It was a battle I had been fighting ever since I started college. I know he did not learn that from Papa.

"Take a seat, ya'll," Lorelei said.

Once we all settled around the large table Papa said grace.

The family feasted on an enormous amount of food: fresh cut strawberries and cantaloupe, cottage cheese delivered that morning from the milk man, and fresh scrambled eggs from Papa's chickens, goat cheese, buttermilk biscuits, gravy, ham, bacon, pancakes and syrup, apple butter and marmalade. Pots of coffee and pitchers of milk were on the table as well.

"Pop, is that goat's milk or cow's milk on the table?" Matt asked.

"I milked that yesterday from the goat, so it's nice and cold. The milk from this morning is not cold yet. I thought the children would like *cold* milk."

"Well, do we have any cream for the coffee?" Matt sounded smug. I got the impression he wasn't partial to goat milk.

Lorelei jumped up to go to the kitchen. "I forgot," and she brought back a small white pitcher in the shape of a cow with its tail the handle and its mouth the spout.

There was so much food that I felt a little queasy just looking at it. The smell of bacon, and ham combined with the smell of maple syrup and strawberries nearly overwhelmed my senses. I instigated conversation so that no one might notice the small amount of food on my plate. Southern folks had a way of showing love through food. If you didn't partake, they felt rejected.

"It's wonderful to sleep in my old room," I said.

"Didja sleep well?" Lorelei asked.

"I did."

"Ah ya stayin wahm up thar in Ohiya?" Matt asked overly exaggerating a southern accent.

"It gets pretty cold in the winter but I guess I've adjusted to it."

"Is there a lot of snow?" Emily asked. Emily, named after our mother, was Matt and Ginny's oldest girl. She had her mother's fair complexion, light brown hair and freckles.

"I'm in the southern part of the state so there is some snow but not as much as up in the northern part," I said.

"I ain't never seen snow fer real. Just p'churs. It must be fun to play in," Danny spoke up. Danny was the middle of the three children. He was not shy in the least. At ten-years-old, he was taller than most boys his age. He had dark skin, eyes, and hair like the Aldridge side of the family.

"Ya'll should come up and visit me next winter. We can play in the snow. There is a wonderful zoo that is open all winter, too. We can go to the zoo. How does that sound?" I asked.

Mary Jane said, "Daddy said you have a convertriple. Can I go for a ride in it?" Mary Jane was seven years old and had a little trouble staying on topic. She, too, was tall, slender and dark but with sparkling green eyes.

Before I could answer, Paul said "MJ, I got to drive it."

"Can I drive it, Aunt Becka?" Mary Jane asked.

"You certainly cannot!" Matt said sternly.

"In a few years I'll let you drive it," I told her.

Matt said "I'd like to come up in the summer and catch a Red Legs game."

I felt the hairs on my neck bristle and just knew what he was going to say next.

"There's a hometown boy pitchin' for em. Remember Josh Stanford?" he asked the entire table. "Hear he's doin pretty good for em."

"I thought that boy would do pretty good in the big leagues," Dr. Stanton added.

Papa interjected "As I remember he was Aaron's age. Don't

think Aaron thought much of him," he looked at Lorelei who remained quiet. Lorelei hadn't usually been introspective whenever Aaron was mentioned. She usually added to the conversation or smiled. This time she looked down.

"Maybe he was jealous," Matt said. "Aaron fancied himself a big league player. Josh was much better."

"I don't think that was it. And I want you to hold your tongue about your brother," Papa said. The way he said it put an end to that. Matt didn't have much to say for the remainder of the morning.

June updated me about anything new that was going on about town, such as the high school adding an indoor swimming pool and a new wing to the public library, which was a gift from the Bradbury family in honor of Judge Bradbury, who passed away two years before. She also loved to gossip about Hollywood movie stars. June Russell tried to look like Jane Russell. She wore her clothes tight to show off her figure. She was an attractive woman in her forties, but her brunette hair was darker than her natural color and her make-up was overdone. It was obvious to almost everyone that June was attracted to my father. To my knowledge, they were not dating and he appeared uncomfortable with her attention.

Dr. Stanton asked me about any research going on at Cincinnati Children's Hospital, and asked me if he could talk to me later about a case that was giving him some concern. He always had a way of making me feel capable and respected as a physician. He and Papa had been friends since the Great War when they served together.

After breakfast, all but Lorelei and Ginny went outside. They remained behind to clear the table and wash the dishes. Dr. Stanton and Matt lit their cigarettes while the children played in the yard. Paul sat at the piano to practice. He had been given a gift of music. Papa, June, and I wandered through the garden and he found a few weeds to pull among the vegetables and flowers. I just wanted to be around him. This was not the time to have the conversation that I planned during my drive home.

Papa thoroughly enjoyed his new goats. They were entertaining as they played and came up to us for attention. June seemed unsure about letting them get close to her. When they started nibbling on her skirt, she went around the front of the house to join the men who were smoking.

"I think I'm going to have my hands full keeping these guys out of the garden. They jump the fence or find things to climb on to get out," Papa said. We enjoyed the silence for a moment as watched them play.

"I am so happy when you come home," he said to me as he hugged me around my shoulders. "I know you are a grown woman and have a career but I worry about you."

"Why do you worry, Papa?" I asked "I'm doing well. Now that I am an attending, I can plan to open my own practice. I'm happy," I tried to sound convincing so that he wouldn't worry.

"I can't help but worry. You're my baby girl. Are you sleeping well? Are you eating well? You hardly had anything for breakfast. But you usually don't eat nutritiously," he said.

"I'm not starving. And I get enough sleep."

"I know you haven't been attending a church. Do you have time for friends? There is more to life than working. Do you have any joy in your life?" he asked pointedly.

I told him all about my new friends, the Sisters, especially Elaine. Her name made him smile.

"Elaine Jayne," he repeated. "And you're playing your cello? I am glad."

"Did Paul tell you that I was at the church when he went over yesterday? I know about the birthday party," I smiled.

"He told me. So you know about your surprise? Maybe you don't know everything," he returned my knowing smile.

"There's more?" I asked, but I knew he wouldn't tell me.
"You'll have to wait and see. Happy birthday, baby girl."

The day was warm and sunny; altogether a beautiful day. It felt good to be home. I had not felt safe in a very long time but here in my father's house I felt safer than anywhere in the world.

"By the way, darlin', you look terrific in slacks." It felt good to have his approval.

For the sake of appearances, when it came time to go to the church, Papa made up an excuse that would get us all to go to the church. He told us that he needed help with decorating the sanctuary for his sermon tomorrow that he had a special treat for everyone. He would not tell us what it was. It was only a ruse for the sake of the others. Of course, no one else but Papa had wished me a happy birthday in the morning.

He drove his blue 1948 Tucker Torpedo and Matt followed in his big new black Caddie. Papa took the road that led us up to the back of the church because everyone else was instructed to park in the front so I wouldn't see all the cars. He opened the back door and went in ahead of us all. I went in after Papa and a room full of people shouted "Happy Birthday" and sang to me "Happy Birthday to you." I was surrounded immediately by people touching and hugging me. Heidi and Wilma had finished decorating the social hall. Tables were covered with pastel table cloths, and fresh cut flowers lined the center of each one. There was so much commotion that it was hard to take it all in.

Finally, Papa got everyone's attention with his booming voice. "Becka, it's always good to have you home. This is your special day and we have a special celebration for you," as he spoke the crowd parted revealing a chair decorated like a throne in the corner of the room. I couldn't help but laugh at the thought of me sitting on a throne. He took my hand and walked me toward the throne. When I got close two girls,

Mindy and Miranda, the Rennold twins, picked up what appeared to be a carpet but was instead a royal robe and placed it on my shoulders. (They took a scene out of the *Wizard of Oz*.) Paul "broke" a flower pot that took the shape of a crown and placed it on my head. Then Papa took me to my place on the throne. I felt thoroughly silly, but happy to play along as they had gone through a lot of trouble for me.

For the next hour, children presented a play, everyone sang a few songs, and I was presented with gifts. Some were silly and some very nice. Dr. Stanton presented me with a brown leather doctor bag complete with apothecary jars, glass syringes and needles, scalpels, thermometers with cases, suture and needles, bandages, a new stethoscope and sphygmomanometer, and a small rubber ice bag.

The biggest surprise was George Anderson. He was home visiting from Africa just in time for my birthday. George professed his love for me when I was ten years old. He told me he would wait for me to marry him even after I told him I didn't want to marry anyone. He arrived after everything else had started and so I didn't notice him for a while.

George stood in the doorway to the kitchen watching me. He smiled when he saw me looking at him. I wanted nothing more than to run over to him and throw my arms around him and apologize for treating him the way I did. We had kept in touch through letters when I went off to school and he went out to the mission field. We lost eye contact when his mother handed him a casserole dish with potholders and pointed for him to take it to the buffet table. She looked up to see me looking at him. There was disapproving look on her face or maybe I just thought there was. I looked away.

Dinner was ready after the other festivities and I was for a little while, and to my relief, not the center of attention. Papa and Dr. Stanton came up to me at this time with another surprise.

"Dr. Aldridge, I have a proposition for you. I have extra examination rooms at the office and space for an additional office. As long as I have been in practice I have never had a partner and have not even considered it before this, but I have been thinking about it since you went off to medical school. I would like you to join me. You could set up a pediatric practice here. We could get you credentialed to admit to Charlotte. There is a growing pediatric department there," he paused for me to give him an answer.

What an honor it would be to work with my mentor. Dr. Stanton was the greatest influence in my decision to become a doctor. Having accepted the Bessimer Fellowship I had made a commitment to Dr. Spence that meant I would be there for the next two years. Then there was the research being done by Dr. Sabin that I had an opportunity in which to assist. My answer would have to be no at this time.

When I told Dr. Stanton this, he looked very disappointed.

"There may never be a later, Becka. I have some health issues myself, and without an heir, I worry that my practice would be without a physician if anything would happen. Please take some time to reconsider my offer," he pleaded with me.

Papa remained silent and his expression gave no indication of what he was thinking. After I reassured Dr. Stanton I would like to think about it some more, the two walked away.

Heidi bounced over and grabbed me by the arm and dragged me over to the food table. It had already been picked over pretty well but it had been a spectacular lay out.

"You have to try some of this soufflé mama made. And this carrot salad! That was made by Mrs. Joyce," she said as she spooned food onto a dish for me. "Your little Lorelei has become quite a cook in her own right. She made this chicken dish that is to die for."

She talked on and on as she continued to load a plate up

for me. I wondered if she did that for her little boy. He didn't look over weight so I assumed she might not have overfed him. But then the entire family was on the slender side, so he may have just had a high metabolism like his mother.

She brought me over to a table and sat me down beside her husband Hank. Heidi went over to gather a plate for herself.

"She's already eaten once. She only eats like this when she is in a family way," Hank offered apologetically.

"She looks lovely," I said, and I meant what I said. Some women have a glow about them when they are pregnant. Heidi truly did radiate. She had always loved children. At one time she entertained the idea of becoming a teacher, but changed her mind when she met Hank.

Hank was three years older than Heidi and I. He moved to Belmont shortly after I left for college to help his brother, Stanley, with his law firm. The business grew so quickly that the firm hired several secretaries, one was Heidi. According to Heidi it was love at first sight. They were married six months after he came to town. The business was still doing quite well.

Hank was average height and build, maybe five feet nine inches tall and 165 pounds and looked very dapper in his business suit. He was probably considered handsome by most women, certainly he was considered handsome to sweet Heidi. She was so very in love with him. But there was something about him that I distrusted. I had no reason to feel this way, of course, he was good to her and his son. There was no gossip and nothing to make me suspicious. It was just an uncomfortable feeling I got when I was around him. It was partly due to the way he looked at me or leaned in close when he talked to me. Maybe I was just imagining it.

When Heidi returned to the table she brought George with her after filling a plate of food for him as well.

George approached me. There was another hug was coming my way.

"When did you get back to the states?" I asked him as he gave me a big bear hug.

"Yesterday," he said, sitting down beside me. "I'll be home for a month before going back to Kenya. We got our cistern dug that I mentioned in my last letter, and started building a school, but the materials take such a long time getting to the area that it could take a year to finish."

George was not as handsome as Hank but I thought he was a very attractive man. He was as tall as my father and lean, brawny like his father. George worked hard and liked to work with his hands doing manual labor but he was also very smart. He was the head of his class in high school beating out my brother Matt by just a few points grade point average. While Matt hated doing manual labor, George got great satisfaction out of it, especially if it was to help another person. I was sure that he still loved me. I could see it in his face.

"There's no medical care there, though, didn't you say?" I asked

"The nearest doctor is seventy-five miles away. They practice very primitive medicine, roots, plants, and chants. They continue to disfigure themselves with rituals. But I do what I can, and teach hygiene. Now we have clean water it helps a great deal," he said proudly, and stopped to take a bite of food.

"Paul says you have a new car, a little sporty deal," Hank said.

"It's a little blue T-bird convertible," I answered.

"Damn, Heidi. I'd like one of those. I could just see us cruisin' around town, but maybe in red," He looked as though he could see it as he passed his outstretched hand across in the air, motioning the movement of a car passing by.

"Hank, if anything we need a family car; maybe a station wagon. With another baby on the way we'll need more room not less," she said popping his dream bubble.

"Still, it would be fun," he said looking at me. I felt he was imagining *me* in the sports car beside him.

In short order, Mrs. Anderson came and sat down on the other side her son. I think she felt she needed to protect him from the one who broke his heart. Despite that, George turned to me and picked up the thread of his previous conversation, said "You should come to Africa with me and practice medicine there. They need doctors in the mission field."

His mother's face expressed a lot of disapproval. "Becka has a job in Cincinnati, George. She made a choice ten years ago. You two went separate ways. And you both chose wisely," she said graciously but the undertones were obvious.

"Mother," George's tone was equally obvious. It said 'stay out of my business' without saying the words.

Loving family and friends, once again descended upon me. It was a welcome disruption.

After the party, and all the happy birthday wishes were repeated, people started filing out to go home. Our family returned to Papa's house. The children, filled with sugar from cake and other desserts bolted out of the car running and playing. They went to Carter's house down the road to play with the children who lived there, leaving the adults to enjoy the gentle quiet of the Saturday afternoon. Papa retreated to the garden to pray.

I went up to my bedroom which remained untouched since I left; preserved just as I left it. It was still my room.

There was always room to lodge a traveler, if necessary. When Lorelei moved in, she shared Aaron's room. When Paul was born he shared the same room with his widowed mother.

When Matt got married and moved out, Paul had his own room.

Benji had shared Papa's room from his birth until he died.

When the whole family was home, as it was now, every bedroom was filled. Lorelei and I shared my room with Matt's daughters. Matt and Ginny used Lorelei's room. Danny stayed in Paul's room

The contingency for unexpected guests was Papa's study. So when Mark Stroup, a missionary, traveling back home to Iowa needed a place to stay to rest for the night Papa was able to accommodate him. He arrived early Saturday evening and planned to leave after services on Sunday. Mark had been doing missions in Haiti. The stories he told were not unlike the ones George had written to me about his experiences in Africa.

Something Mark said struck a chord in me. He was going back home to get married and then his wife would join him in the mission field.

"There is such mistrust among the women there for a single white man. My wife will bring out little more trust from them."

George had never said as much but I wondered if he was experiencing any such issues.

CHAPTER 11

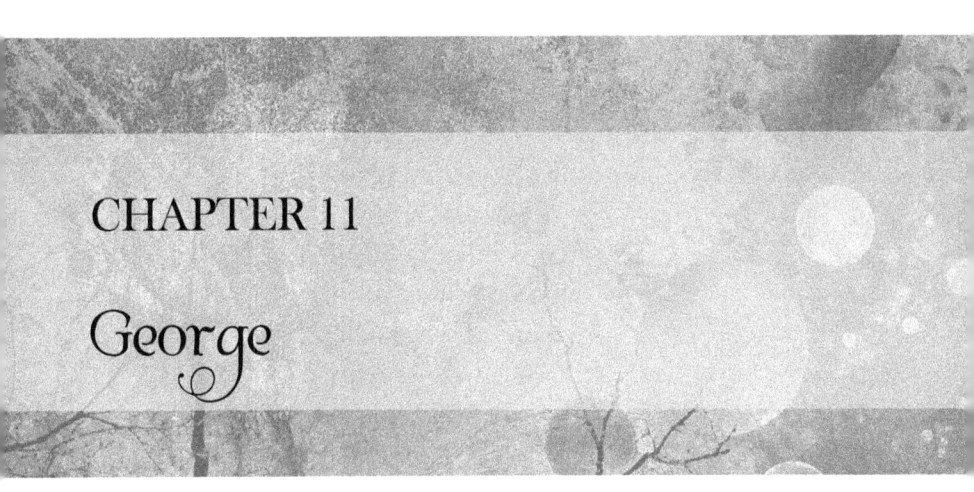

George

Sunday, after church, a flurry of visitors kept everything hopping. The entire family, all home together, drew friends, some of whom we hadn't seen for quite a while. Dozens of people, whose friendships were built over more than twenty years, passed in and out of our front door.

In 1934 our little family moved to Belmont, just outside of Charlotte. We moved 100 miles away from Gammy and Pappy and all the family I had known.

The Living Water Church hired Papa to be their pastor after the previous pastor passed away. The church, immensely larger than the one he pastored in Rock Creek, had a sanctuary that seemed cavernous to me. I counted three columns of pews, ten in each row with enough room for ten people each and a balcony. The sheer size of the empty sanctuary intimidated me, but I trembled that first Sunday service when people filled those pews.

Papa had instructed us to sit in the front row in the left section. He had familiarized himself with member seating preferences and placed us up front with Mr. and Mrs. Anderson whom he had met earlier in the week.

Heidi Anderson was my age. She was friendly and 'girly' while I, on the other hand, was shy and clumsy. She smiled a lot and I tended to cling to my Papa and try to hide. Mr. Anderson sat on the aisle seat next to his mother Mrs. Langley (who was widowed twice), then George on the right side of Mrs. Anderson, and then Heidi and me on her left side. Benji was carried to the pew and sat next to me in a special seat made for him, Matt was seated on the other side of Benji and Aaron at the end of the row. Benji's wheel chair was parked in the back of the sanctuary.

When Papa took his place behind the pulpit, instead of looking dwarfed by the large chancel area, he seemed larger than life to me. I knew he belonged there and I belonged to him, and so I belonged there, too. I was no longer afraid.

The next week Heidi introduced me to everyone at school as her best friend. I accepted the honor without a second thought. At Rock Creek, my closest friends were my older cousins.

The next Saturday she convinced her mother to give a tea party for me with other girls from church. It was the whole of our Sunday school class, six girls. Heidi told George that he was not to bother the girls at the party. It was for girls only. But he kept finding ways to intrude on Heidi's shindig.

Once he helped his mother by bringing in a tray of little cakes she had made. Next, he had to ask Heidi a "very important question" and called her aside. This made her very angry. He accidentally lobbed his baseball into the garden where we were having our tea party, which of course, he had to retrieve.

I had to laugh when he began jumping off the tree swing as he swung higher and higher. He had succeeded in getting all the girl's attention just as he had set off to do, and infuriating his little sister.

"Just ignore him," Heidi instructed us.

"But he's just so funny," I said. My attempt to defend him didn't faze her in the least.

"Please just try to ignore him. He's just trying to make me mad."

Later, I found out that it wasn't the case. He wasn't trying to make her angry but instead he was trying to get my attention, which he did.

George began talking to me more, and more, seeking me out before and after church. When Mrs. Anderson started separating Heidi and I during service because we got too giggly or talkative, my new pew partner was George. Not only didn't I mind but sometimes I *acted up* on purpose. George would half smile – not looking in my direction, but keeping his eyes straight on the preacher. But I noticed his smile. When we were older, he would take hold of my hand.

Aaron didn't like the fact that George paid so much attention to me. Aaron had several 'talks' with George about it and one time it lead up to a pushing match. Papa stepped in and broke it up and made Aaron apologize to George, which didn't set well with Aaron; ever! He always held a grudge after that.

George was the very opposite of my brother. He was kind and slow to anger and he was forgiving.

After Papa's talk with Aaron, Aaron tolerated George. They were placed in situations almost daily where they had to talk to each other, work together or study together.

The Anderson "men" and the Aldridge "men" and the other church men and boys formed a community that did a lot together. They helped neighbors dig wells, patch barns, paint the church or make props for the children's programs, or anything else that one of them might need done. Once or twice a year they would go on a camping or fishing trip together.

Aaron and George often worked side by side and seemed

to get along. But if Matt or I asked Aaron about George his answer would always be negative.

On the other hand, Matt and George became close friends. They would laugh and tease each other all the time, both having a fun-loving side and both a serious side. George knew early on that he wanted to serve God. Matt knew early on that he liked money and what money could buy; much to Papa's chagrin. But apparently there were enough common interests that they bonded in a way that they kept each other in balance.

When, years later, George proposed to me and I turned him down, Matt was very angry with me.

"You've always known how George felt about you. This doesn't make any sense, Becka. I coulda sworn that you loved him back all these years."

Matt was right. I did love George and now as we walked down the road along the creek I knew I still loved him and that I didn't deserve him.

CHAPTER 12

Papa's Grace

A few nights later Papa and I sat on the porch swing. The night was hot and still. The house was empty as everyone else had gone to the movies to see the new picture show *Moby Dick*. Papa had turned off the porch light so that moths, mosquitoes and June bugs would not buzz around our heads. The soft light from inside the house illuminated his face. Father's face; time worn with parentheses around his mouth, high cheekbones marking his heritage, and liquid dark brown eyes under thick eyebrows, looked serene in the soft glow of the lamp in the window. It was a face that I loved my whole life.

We sat in blissful quiet for quite some time. Then he began the conversation I dreaded.

"So, Becka, Sweetie why aren't you going to church?"

After a brief discussion about why I wasn't attending church in Cincinnati he came directly to the point. "Becka, are you angry at God?" he asked point blank.

I looked away briefly and then looking him straight in the eyes I answered "Yes."

I found myself praying to a God for the second time that

I hadn't spoken to in a very long time asking for the words to tell my father what I needed to say. Papa sat very straight, his posture nearly rigid, but his facial expression did not change. He was quiet.

Please don't let him stop loving me, I prayed.

Papa spoke next "We have lost a lot haven't we?" he said gently.

"Yes, we have, but that's not the reason I'm angry. Well, maybe that is part of it. Papa, earlier this year, I had to take care of a little girl who was nearly beaten to death by her stepfather," I thought of Lorelei and I'm sure Papa did too. "He raped her Papa," I started to cry but regained my composure. "How can God let all this happen? I've seen so many little ones who suffer so much. Benji, and Lorelei…and me," I had to stop before I broke down altogether.

As he always had whenever I was hurting Papa leaned over and hugged me. Holding me to his chest, he said "Talk to me, Sweetheart."

I took a deep breath and composed myself in his embrace. He smelled of straw and perspiration and the soil from the garden he had been working in earlier.

"I have to tell you something, Papa," I pulled myself away and he sat quietly next to me.

"Do you remember the Independence Day Picnic when I was twelve-years-old?"

He looked into my eyes but did not speak.

"I…" hesitation "something awful happened. Someone hurt me." There was no need to mention who. Nothing could be done now. Papa's eyebrows knitted into a furrow and his mouth turned down at the corners. He knew what I meant when I said someone 'hurt' me.

Papa was thoughtful for a moment and then spoke "Did he threaten you, too? Did he tell if you told anyone he would do something else?" he asked knowingly.

I nodded my head. "He said it was my fault and that you would lose your church if folks knew I was such a wicked girl."

"I am so sorry, Baby Girl. I'm sorry it happened. I'm sorry I couldn't prevent it from happening in the first place. I'm sorry I didn't know."

There it was. The trigger to my pent up anger.

"Why didn't you know? I changed. I needed you to see I was different. I was scared all of the time. I didn't play anymore. I didn't eat." Tears flowed freely.

Papa recoiled. Hurt and sadness plain as day on his face. My anger changed to pity.

"I'm sorry, Papa. I'm sorry," I said out loud and thought to myself *don't hate me*. "I knew you couldn't have known. I didn't tell you. How could you know?"

"I saw the light disappear from your eyes," Papa blinked several times and stared out into the darkness of the trees.

Tears blurred my vision, but I could see the yellow glow of the lightening bugs brighten and then dim out of sight, temporarily leaving the void that much darker. Here and there another began to brighten.

He continued after an interminable silence, "You wouldn't tell me what happened. When I got nowhere, I had Aaron check around. He wouldn't tell me either, but I knew he took care of it. He told me that much."

I had no recollection of Papa asking me what happened. What else had I erased from my memory?

"I should have made you tell me, but I didn't know how. Boys are different. In a way, they were easier to raise," then he stopped and looked me in the eyes, "Not that you were ever any trouble, Sugar Pie. It's just that you were…fragile," Papa gently rubbed my cheek. "After that, you were almost never out of my sight and when you were someone I trusted was always watching over you."

Yes. Yes. I thought. *There were times that I wish I could get away from everyone's watchful eyes.* It dawned on me that Aaron walking me home was because Papa had set him onto it.

"All this time I thought...I don't know what I thought. I've been so hurt that you weren't there to protect me, even though I knew that made no sense. But you were, weren't you? I've let what happen drive me. I still feel like I can't be good enough, or clean enough or worthy to be loved. I love you Papa and I know you love me," I said

"I love you more than life," he said.

He held me close as we sat on the porch swing. There was a slight dampness to his shirt when I laid my face against his chest. It brought back the feeling of his embrace when I was a child. He was strong and I felt small, but safe.

I was so thankful that we were alone. I cried freely unashamed of my tears. Papa cried too.

There were only three times in my life that I remember Papa crying.

The first was a distant but very clear memory. The morning Mama died. Aaron had gotten me out of bed and dressed me. We were at Gammy's house and I was three years old. Aaron was a little rough and impatient with me. He tied my shoes so tightly that they hurt. I untied them. He sat me down hard on the blanket chest and retied my shoes even tighter.

When we went downstairs there were a lot of people in the house and more standing outside. Everyone looked very sad.

Aaron took me into the kitchen to Gammy. Aunt Glory and Aunt Patsy and several cousins were cooking for a crowd. They danced around each other in coordinated movements. One lifting the pan of biscuits high while another bent down to move a pot to the kitchen counter. The fragrance of fresh coffee brewing on the stove was always in Gammy's kitchen. Fatback sizzled on the griddle and a pot of pinto beans boiled on the stove. These memories were vivid and unforgettable.

Gammy pulled me to her breast and squeezed me very tightly. She was soft and smelled like buttermilk. Between my tightly tied shoes and Gammy's tight bear hug I felt very afraid. Tears were trailing down her face.

It was then that she told me Mama had gone to be with Jesus, but Jesus gave me a baby brother.

Matthew was brought in next by Aaron. He was crying but Aaron was stone faced. Shortly we were shuttled into the room with all the people. They touched or kissed me and hugged me. I was swallowed up in a sea of people.

All my aunts and uncles and cousins were there, and church people, too. Papa came in later. He sat down on the arm chair and motioned for us to come over. Papa didn't speak. He just embraced all three of us and buried his head in Aaron's chest but he couldn't speak. He cried for a long time, so did Matt and I. Aaron did not cry. I can't recall a single time that Aaron cried. Not even at Mama's funeral

The next time I saw Papa cry was when he got the telegram from the War Department telling us Aaron had been killed in action.

He was at the pulpit on a Wednesday evening. The telegram delivery boy came in and asked for "Mrs. Aaron Aldridge." Of course, everyone knew what that meant.

Papa stepped down from the pulpit and held Lorelei close. She wept openly. He let tears come but did not make a sound.

When Benji died I did not see Papa cry. He delivered the service and I understood why he didn't cry. He said that Benji was finally safe in his mother's arms.

"We got to hold him in our arms and laugh when he laughed. Now his mother will keep him in her arms until we are all together again. Mama, Aaron and Benji were all in heaven with Jesus and we will all be reunited." He rejoiced in that knowledge.

Now Papa cried, right along with me.

After the crying subsided I pulled up the courage to ask him "Papa, how did you get through everything that you've been through?"

"What choice is there? Who am I that it shouldn't happen to me and should happen to someone else?" he looked down the road at nothing. "Life isn't meant to be fair. If everything was perfect all the time there wouldn't be a need for God. Would there?"

"What do you mean? Why shouldn't life be fair? You know some people who never suffer adversity. They have everything they want and no bad stuff happens to them. Some of them don't even have faith in God. There are some bad people who have always had nearly perfect lives. And you have served Him all your life and all these awful things have happened to you. I don't understand," I pleaded for help to understand the injustice.

"You know the story of how my mother died. I think I have told you that she had such an unshakable faith in Jesus, that from the time she died, I never had a doubt where she went and that I would be with her again one day. I have had peace through all of these losses but it's only been through Jesus. St. Paul, the apostle called it 'The peace that surpasses understanding.' I know that God loves my mother, he loves Marie, he loves your mother, he loves Aaron and Benji more than even I do. He loves them more than even you do," he said.

"What makes you think that, Papa? He has let all these bad things happen to them," I argued.

"I know it because he sent his son to take all our sins upon himself and be crucified for us. I don't think I could sacrifice a child of mine to save someone else. Jesus was sinless and took our sins upon himself. Because of that, God accepts all who believe. We get to be with him in heaven. We get to be with your mother, Marie, my first wife, Aaron, Benji, your grandmother and grandfather. There is nothing that can happen in this life that is worse than being separated from him for eternity. Something else you need to know, Sweetheart, God doesn't cause all these bad things to happen. There is evil in this world because Satan is causing it. People have free will to choose to do good or evil, like the boy who hurt you. But God will forgive anyone who confesses and repents. These are his promises and He is the only one who can be trusted to keep all his promises."

"So, He will forgive Josh? If you met the men who killed your mother, would you be able to forgive him?" the prospect of that was unimaginable.

"I turned that over to the Lord years ago. I did meet them. They were caught, tried and convicted. I wrote them some letters when they were in prison. Only one wrote back. So I wrote again and I told him that I forgave him and hoped that he got to know the Lord, so that God would forgive him as well. He wrote me back several times. At first the letters were defensive and angry at his lawyers, but over time he did come to know Jesus and was saved. I wrote him that I was sure my mother would welcome him in heaven."

"Good, Papa. I'm not sure that I could do that. Sister Elaine told me the same thing. She said that I needed to forgive him for my own good."

"She is wise. You should keep her counsel. You forgive him not for him, but because you can start to let it go. Can we pray?" he asked me.

"Alright." I acquiesced.

We sat there and bowed our heads.

"Father, You are Good. You are not capable of evil. Your love for us is true and you want good for us. My daughter has been hurting for a long time. With Your help she will heal. Bless her with the peace you have given me. Help her to know that she is blameless in what happened to her. Bring her back to you. Call her name so that she will seek you out. You have given me such a blessing in her. I know pride in self is sinful, but she is my pride. I ask this in Jesus name. Amen"

I never stopped loving my father but that love had become dulled and rote. I had imposed a division between Papa and myself. Now with this burden lifted off my shoulders that relationship was closer than ever. Just putting into words the ridiculous subconscious blame I held onto so tightly allowed me to let go of all the blame and anger.

Shortly afterward, the crowd came back from the movie. No one could tell we had been crying. Everyone was talking at once about what they had seen. They joined us on the front porch. I asked questions about the movie. It had been such a long time since I had read the book that I resolved to read it again after hearing their account.

After the conversation died down a bit, Papa went inside and got his guitar and Paul's fiddle. The violin had been his father's. When Matt saw Papa bringing out the instruments, he went to his car and pulled his guitar and tambourine from the trunk. He gave the tambourine to Danny. While Papa went inside, George boldly took Papa's place beside me on the swing.

"What do you want to hear?" Papa asked the folks as he sat on the step, never mentioning his lost spot on the swing.

"Something upbeat," Ginny said. "How about 'When the Saints Go Marching In?'"

Papa started off and everyone fell in playing, singing, and clapping. Even though it wasn't rehearsed, it sounded like beautiful harmony to me. "Old Time Religion," "Just a Closer Walk with Thee," " Victory in Jesus," " He Lives," " What A Friend We Have In Jesus." We sang one after another of the old familiar hymns.

It was getting late and the children were getting tired.

Ginny excused herself to put them to bed and nearly everyone else followed suit. George and I stayed behind on the swing. It was a warm, lovely summer night and I felt I could stay sitting close to George all night.

"Becka?" George nearly whispered.

"Humm?"

"I've loved you since we were kids. I'll never not love you." he said tenderly

"I know," I whispered back.

"Never."

"I know."

He held me closer and I leaned my head on his shoulder.

He did not attempt to kiss me. I'm sure he remembered, just as I did the first and last time he kissed me. It was the summer after I graduated from high school and he was home from college on summer break. He walked me home after choir practice on a night much like tonight. I remember a tender sweet kiss but a blind panic arose up in me so strongly that I pushed him away and started to run home. I stumbled and my heart was racing and I could barely breathe. George caught me before I could fall, but I tried to hit him several times. He hugged me closer to keep me from hitting him.

"Let me go," I shouted repeatedly.

"OK, just don't…don't run away," he stammered.

"Just let me go," I snapped.

George apologized. "I will never hurt you," he said.

It took me some time to calm down enough to even speak to him.

"I can't," I whined.

"I won't ever do that again without asking first," then he thought more of it and added "In fact, you'll have to kiss me if it's to happen at all."

"I just can't," was my only response.

Now years later, I wondered if I could kiss him without that familiar old panic inside. I knew I still wasn't ready. I didn't know if that day would ever come. So, once again I urged him to find another, and again he refused.

CHAPTER 13
Sully

The next day was Wednesday. Matt, Ginny and the children packed their car up that morning to return home.

Before they left we all drove over to the cemetery to lay flowers on Benji's and Aaron's graves. M.J. sang a sweet little song to Benji and muttered "I miss you, Uncle Benji."

Lorelei whispered "I still love you," to Aaron's headstone.

Images of eighteen year old Benji played in my mind. Images of his contorted little body lying on a blanket on the grass one hot summer day as little Mary Jane's tiny baby fingers touched his face and the two of them were laughing. And as a toddler, little MJ dressed in her Sunday dress feeding Benji mashed bananas with a spoon, getting food all down the front of both of them both laughing so sweetly. Also, I remembered an image of her crying inconsolably at his funeral. They had a deep connection that I hope will keep him alive long after Papa, Matt and I are gone.

Papa recited the 23rd Psalm over the graves before we left the cemetery.

From there, we all said goodbye and I embraced my only

remaining brother for a long, long time. I didn't want to let him go. He had moist eyes as he smiled at me and kissed my cheek.

As Papa drove us home he asked Lorelei "Why don't you invite Sully over for dinner tonight before service?"

Lorelei bristled and blinked quickly "Because!"

"Because?" Papa asked.

"Just…just because," she barked. I could tell she was embarrassed by the question.

Paul sat quietly with me in the back seat casting his gaze from Papa to his mother.

There was something going on that Lorelei didn't want to discuss, so I decided I would ask Papa later when we were alone. But he wouldn't let it drop.

"Well. I will call him then," he teased.

"No, you won't."

"OK, then. I won't," he said smiling.

I caught Paul's attention and raised my eyebrows in question. Paul just shrugged his shoulders and shook his head.

Arthur Densmore Sullivan was a classmate and sometimes friend of Aaron. They would get into mischief together, or fight and then become friends again. Sully joined the Army at the same time as Aaron, but Sully returned home, and Aaron never came back.

I knew that Sully had become an over-the-road trucker and after a few years started his own successful trucking business. What I didn't know was that he was attempting to court Lorelei.

The car got quiet and we all retreated into our own thoughts. Sometimes, I kept so busy at the hospital I forgot how homesick I could get.

Driving home from the cemetery I noticed how different even the air felt in North Carolina. It was fresher and sweeter. The grass was greener, more fragrant. The flowers were more beautiful. There was a heavy tugging at my heart, knowing that I would again have to leave the warmth of my family and friends and return to a more isolated, numb life in a big, sometimes unfeeling city where I felt alone. But, the city was, at least for me, beginning to change. Two friends, that I felt a bond with, waited for me back in Cincinnati. Sister Elaine and Sophie were there for me. I wanted to be there for them as well.

I would be returning in one week, so I needed to soak up all the love I could in this place to sustain me, until I could come back. Whenever that would be, I was uncertain.

Papa pulled the car up into the yard in front of the house. No one had said a word for a mile, but there wasn't a sense of lingering frustration. It was a rare occasion that Lorelei got irritated, but anytime she did, it was short lived. She never hung onto it.

As soon as we arrived home we noticed a note stuck to the screen door addressed to Pastor Aldridge. He read the note and told us that he had to go to the hospital in Charlotte. One of his parishioners needed him. He let Lorelei know that he might miss dinner and told us not to wait but that he would be home before the night's services.

There were only a few instances that I could remember when Papa had to miss a service, but there were quite a few family and holiday dinners he missed because duty called him away.

He never told us before he left, why he was needed. So we learned early not to ask. When he came back he might tell us, when he felt it was alright to share. As a physician I learned the importance of keeping confidences.

While Lorelei made dinner, Paul and I read. Papa had a copy of Melville's *Moby Dick* on the shelf.

Call me Ishmael.
Some years ago-

never mind how long
having little or no money in my purse…[1]

The story began so simply, yet I was transported in my imagination to a harbor town by the ocean; walking down gritty streets; passing gray buildings, with the smell of the salty sea in my nostrils.

Reading was one of my greatest pleasures. I was so deeply absorbed that I was oblivious to anything going on around me, until Paul touched my shoulder

When I looked up there was a man standing beside him smiling at me.

"Just like when you were a kid. Your nose was always in a book," he said.

From his response, I must have had a bewildered expression on my face.

"You don't remember me. Do you?" he laughed.

"I'm…I'm sorry. You look fam…" I stuttered.

"Sully," he interrupted. "I was a friend of Aaron's," he puffed out his chest. "I know it's been a long time. Don't think I seen you since I joined the Army. Prolly changed a lot. I know you shore have," he said with a big grin.

"Arthur Sullivan. What a coincidence," I responded. "Your name came up earlier today, and here you are."

I got out of my chair and gave him a hug, which I think surprised both of us.

"With that kind of reception I should come visit every day."

"What brings you by?" My question sounded sincerely innocent but I suspected he had come to see Lorelei.

"Hello Sully," Lorelei tried to sound casual. But the fact that she was wearing lipstick when she came from the hallway

---

[1] Moby Dick, Or The Whale, Herman Melville, New York, Charles Scribner's Sons, 1902

told me she had done a little primping. She usually didn't wear lipstick. I suspect she heard his truck pull up into the yard.

Her embarrassment in the car earlier may have been genuine in front of Papa. It was obvious now that she was flattered by Sully's interest in her.

"Hello, sweet Lorelei," Sully beamed. "How are you today?"

"Fair to middlin'," she said.

"Well, you're lookin' better than just fair to middlin'. You're lookin' pretty fine."

She blushed.

"How about if you stay to dinner? You know I always make too much," she said.

"Yeah," Paul chimed in "Ham and biscuits and sweet potatoes. Good stuff," he drew out the word good for emphasis

It seemed Paul didn't object to his mother's suitor. He later, told me that he liked Sully.

"He's down-to-earth. And he makes Mama smile. I like to see her smile," he said.

We all did. She had the smile of an angel.

In his younger days, Sully was small, thin and scrappy. He was always in need of a haircut. While he hadn't gotten much taller than I remembered he was no longer skinny. A round, ruddy face and neatly trimmed thinning hair softened that hard youthful edge, that I remembered. He wore a clean plaid cotton button down shirt with a solid color brown tie that matched the brown in the plaid. His demeanor had changed as well. He no longer had that defiant air that both he and Aaron shared. He was self-assured but not arrogant. Successful in his business, but what surprised me most of all, he was humble. Sully was hard not to like. Over dinner he told me about how he got started in business. He was a former Teamster and his employees are all union drivers.

"There is a need for union and the Teamsters. They do a

lot of good. During the War they built roads and bridges in Europe and the Pacific that helped the allies win the War. I don't think of them as the enemy and I don't think my guys see me that way, either."

About an hour later, it was time to start getting ready for church. Lorelei asked Sully if he would like to go to church with us.

He politely declined. Lorelei was very disappointed. "Didn't think so, but I'm not going to stop asking you."

I sensed this may have been why she was hesitant to go out with him. Later I learned that Sully didn't go to any church. "I'll pray for you," She smiled

"God knows, I need all the prayers I can get," he smiled back.

Shortly after Sully left, Papa came home. He was quiet and serious.

"Somethin' happen, Papaw?" Paul asked.

"Mr. Jenkins passed away," he said.

It wasn't surprising that Mr. Jenkins died. He was quite old, and had been sick for a long time.

"I'm sorry, Becka. The funeral will be Saturday and I'll be needed by the Jenkins' quite a bit. Ms. Jenkins is getting pretty senile and she and her daughter are having a hard time," he explained

I could tell, he was disappointed that he couldn't spend the time with me.

"It's alright, Papa. They need you."

CHAPTER 14
Much on Forgiveness

At the Wednesday night service, I sat by Heidi and Hank. She invited me to spend the entire next day with her.

The message of Papa's sermon was about Grace; God's undeserved forgiveness of us all. We sang the Fannie Crosby song "Saved by Grace" lead by Paul playing the piano. "And I shall see Him face to face, and tell the story –saved by Grace. And I shall see Him face to face, and tell the story save by Grace"

Papa stood tall behind the pulpit. His voice was strong and certain.

"Some of you know the story of how my mother died when I was a young boy. Most of you don't," he began. "Late one night Mother and I were walking home from her job; she worked at a cotton mill, when she was attacked by three men who didn't like that her son was half Indian. They beat her and threw her off an embankment and left her to die.

"She was a good God-fearing woman who always tried to do good. She was kind and gentle, generous and loving. She taught me that God loved me. He loved us enough to send

His son to die to save us. But after she died, I forgot that He loved me. I was more than just a difficult child. I was unruly, strong willed, and defiant. In the meantime, my Uncle Samuel who had been lost became saved. He was trying to raise me, but nearly at his wits end. Once he got saved I could see my mother through him. He and his wife and their church wouldn't give up on me. They helped me find my way back to Jesus. There were some hard lessons to learn.

"The men who killed my mother were serving time in jail for her murder. Uncle Samuel encouraged me to write to them. Imagine that! I did not want to do it. What could I possibly have to say to them? But Uncle Samuel was a very wise man. When I sat down to write those letters the words I wanted to put to paper, words full of anger and hate – yes hate - refused to be written down. Instead Jesus' words filled my head.

"In Matthew 5: 39–48, Jesus said, "But I say unto you, that ye resist no evil but whosoever shall smite you on the right cheek, turn to him the other also. And if any man will sue thee at the law and take away thy coat, let him have thy cloak also. And whosoever shall compel thee to go a mile, go with him twain. Ye have heard that it hath been said Thou shalt love thy neighbor and hate thine enemy. But I say unto you, love your enemies, bless them that curse you, do good to them that hate you, and pray for them which despitefully use you and persecute you."

Papa continued, "Even at that young age, I knew that those words went beyond one who strikes you on the face, or takes your shirt, or makes you walk a mile. Those words encompassed even the most egregious offenses.

"But also in Proverbs 25: verses 21 and 22 Solomon wrote 'If thine enemy be hungry, give him bread to eat; and if he be thirsty, give him water to drink: For thou shalt heap coals of fire upon his head, and the Lord shall reward thee.' I have to confess that I liked the idea of heaping coals of fire on their heads. So I was still angry when I wrote the letters but no words of hatred were written, but neither were words of forgiveness. I wrote to them about how their actions had affected my life and how much I missed my mother. I wrote to them about the kind of person she was. How she worked hard to provide for us. And that she never raised her hand to me. She went out of her way to help other people, even strangers.

"So Jesus continued in Matthew why we must forgive our enemies. 'That ye may be the children of your Father which is in heaven: for he maketh his sun to rise on the evil and on the good, and sendeth rain on the just and the unjust. For if ye love them which love you, what reward have ye? Do not even the publicans the same? And if ye salute your brethren only, what do ye more than others? Do not even the publicans so? Be ye therefore perfect, even as your Father which is in heaven is perfect.'

"We forgive them because we belong to Him. Through Him, we can forgive even horrible things.

"Only one of the three men wrote back to me at that time. He didn't admit guilt or complicity in the crime. He denied that he had any part of if, and he wrote of how horrible prison was. Some parts of his letter were blacked out. I suppose all incoming and outgoing mail was censored. But he did say one thing, one small phrase that impressed me. He wrote 'Your mother must have been a saint.' I had intended to send only one letter to each man because that is what Uncle Samuel said I must do. My obligation was met. But because of what he wrote back I continued to correspond with him. I would write about what I was learning in church and in Bible study. One time he asked me if I would send him a Bible. I sent it. I also let him know that I forgave him. Indeed, I had.

"I kept all of his letters. They are tied in a bundle and remain in my Bible even now. In one of his letters, after years of back and forth correspondence, he finally admitted what he had done and told me how because of my letters that he knew that God could forgive him.

"It is only through God's Grace and mercy that we have the strength to forgive. I forgave all three men, not just the one who admitted what he had done; not only the one who wanted forgiveness. Because of that forgiveness, I was able to let go of the things that kept me in chains…anger, hate, self-pity, self-blame, despair. People, God's instructions are simple and they are wise, but they are not easy. He can help you get there if you ask Him. All you have to do is surrender it all to Him. Pray, my friends. I will pray for and with anyone who wishes. Come to the rail and kneel with me and we can ask Him the way to this peace."

I tried to resist the alter call but went u, compelled by a force I later understood. The Holy Spirit pulled many of us up to the front of the church that Wednesday evening.

Papa prayed for all people who are hurt and hold onto hurt and so can't move on. He prayed with me.

CHAPTER 15
Heidi

Heidi was hanging sheets on the line when I came to visit. Mitch played with a little yellow bulldozer in a sandbox, close to his mother.

"Good morning, Mrs. Becker," I called out as I rounded the back of the house, "And good morning, Mr. Mitch."

Mitch jumped to his feet and ran over to me. Heidi smiled and laughed at him.

"Wash day?" I asked.

"Things get ahead of me a little these days. I had intended to have this done before you came over. I'm not the housekeeper my mama is," she said apologetically.

"I'm ashamed to admit, I'm not a housekeeper at all. My little apartment isn't hard to keep tidy but it's not something I enjoy. I have to say I love coming home and having Lorelei spoil me."

"Did you come to the front door? I'm sorry I didn't hear you."

I replied, "That's alright. When you didn't come to the door I figured we're friends enough that I can come to the back door."

"Of course."

She finished hanging up the sheets and took me inside to show me their new home. It was large and beautiful. It could have been torn from the pages of *House Beautiful*. Everything was immaculate, except for a play area just for Mitch, which was strewn with toys. There were four bedrooms, two bathrooms, a mud room, a den, a living room, and kitchen, dining room, and a basement. Most houses in Belmont did not have basements. Heidi and Hank had every modern convenience, such as a dishwasher, huge refrigerator, a large washing machine and dryer.

"Why are you hanging clothes outside when you have this nice dryer?" I asked

"We like the smell of sheets off the line."

"Your home is absolutely beautiful, Heidi"

"I am happy with it. Have you had breakfast, Becka? I can make you something," she said.

"I have, thank you."

"How about a cup of coffee, then?" she asked.

"If you have some already made. I don't want you to go to any trouble."

"It will only take a few minutes."

We sat sipping our steaming coffee. Mitch sat at the table perched atop telephone books.

"I'm too big for a high chair," he asserted.

"That you are, big man," I agreed.

He also thought he was big enough to drink coffee with the grown-ups, but his mother disagreed and Mitch lost the argument.

My friend looked gaunt and exhausted. There were dark circles under her eyes and her head tilted to one side as if it were too heavy to lift.

"How are you feeling today?" I inquired.

"Very well," she smiled, taking much effort to look perky.

I dropped the inquiry, although I was concerned about my friend.

"I brought you a gift," I had been carrying it in a bag and she was too proper to ask what was in the bag.

"That is so thoughtful. Just like you," she said, as she took my gift.

"What are you hoping for, a boy or a girl?" I asked.

Her expression fell. She hesitated to open her gift. It was not the response I expected.

"I just want a healthy baby," she spoke seriously. She looked at the little one in the chair beside her. "Mitchy is such a blessing. How do you prepare for one that isn't healthy?"

I was beginning to worry that something might be wrong. Heidi was not herself

"It doesn't make sense to worry about something that might or might not happen. You're going to love this baby, right? Of, course you will."

She made another effort at smiling while still holding onto her unopened present.

Mitch piped up "Whas in ur pwesent, Mama?"

"Well, let's find out," she perked up and carefully removed the ribbon and wrapping from the box. Inside the box was a package of cloth diapers, diaper pins, and seven receiving blankets in soft pastels. The blankets were folded to look like a bouquet of flowers. I had paid one of the nurses who had made these for others to create this for me before I left Cincinnati. There was also a certificate entitling the bearer to one year of free diaper service out of Charlotte. This I had arranged through a series of long distance telephone calls and through the postal service while I was still in Cincinnati.

"Oh my! That is extravagant. Especially for a home maker," she said.

I interjected "A very busy homemaker with two children. They will come out twice a week to pick up the soiled diapers and leave you fresh clean ones."

"I will be so spoiled," she gushed.

"You won't have time to be spoiled, darling. This will be one less thing you have to worry about."

Mitch was impressed with the blanket bouquet but only for an instant. "Ooh, soft, Mama," but no sooner had the words come from his mouth than he ran off to get his own soft but battered blanket.

"Dis one's mine," he boasted.

"Very nice," I exaggerated the words.

"You can hold it," he then threw it on my lap and ran off again, this time to play with some building blocks on the living room floor.

"This is so lovely, Becka. I can't tell you how much I appreciate it. I don't know anyone who has had a diaper service before. I think I'll be the envy of the neighborhood," she sipped her coffee. "I've just been so very tired lately. The joy of it all…I'm just so tired," she trailed off.

"Has the doctor said anything that has caused you to worry?" I asked bluntly.

"It's not anything he said. It's just how he says things. The kinds of questions he asks. The way he looks at me," another sigh.

"You can ask him, dear. Have you asked him if there is something he is concerned about?"

"No. I'm afraid of what he might say," her eyes brimmed with tears.

Things got quiet for a moment. Heidi the "chatterbox," who was never at a loss for words, withdrew. She was introspective. She was scared.

There were many thoughts that came to my mind that at first seemed like words of comfort but I did not utter them, because as I thought more on each one it would not have been a comfort at all.

I just reached across and took both of her hands in mine. It was a small thing I saw Sister Elaine do that had meant a lot to me. "I'm here for you. And if you need me, call me and I'll come," I didn't know how I would make it happen but I meant it.

We watched Mitch play for a while. Then we picked up our conversation. She talked about her mother, and father, about Mitch and Hank. Her mood lightened more and more as we talked.

When it got to be lunch time her energy begin to wane. I insisted on taking them to lunch in town. She tried to resist but she was out numbered when Mitch threw in his vote.

Herbie's Diner didn't have a large menu but everything on it was delicious. His ground steak sandwich was my favorite. We saw quite a few people we knew in the diner. The bank, the Post Office and most business offices closed for lunch. Factories and mills let workers leave for the lunch hour. In fact, all the restaurants and eateries were very busy between 11:30 and 1:00pm. Some were ONLY open for lunch and breakfast.

Conversations and playful banter took place across the tables. Strangers were treated like friends, and friends like family. I got to see and talk to folks I had known most of my life, but that I hadn't seen since coming home. While it was still a small town, the world within it went beyond family and our church.

Belmont had a census of 2,100 residents. So I didn't know everyone by name, but everyone I saw at least looked familiar. Something, however, felt different. In the past there was a sense that everyone I saw somehow knew that I was a sinner. I sensed that they judged me and found me lacking. I did not measure up to the standard. But now, unexplainably, that foreboding was gone. There was a feeling of ease. Almost acceptance, or at least regard.

"May I join you?" Sully begged. He appeared out of the crowd. Ours was the only table with an empty seat. It would be rude to refuse.

"Of course, Mr. Sullivan. Do you know my dear friend, Heidi?"

I know Mrs. Becker. How are you?" he smiled at Heidi.

"Very well, thank you."

"And young Mr. Becker," Sully extended his hand to Mitch. The little gentleman knew what to do and shook the extended hand shyly.

"How are you, Mr. Sullivan?" Heidi asked

"Sully, please!" he requested.

"Sully," she repeated.

"The day is beautiful. Business is good, AND I am in the company of two beautiful southern ladies. What more could a man ask? Right, Mitch?" he spoke loudly to be heard above the noise of the crowded restaurant.

Mitch clearly didn't understand the question but was happy to be included in the conversation.

"Yep," he answered.

Shortly we placed our order. At once when the soda pops in throw away cups were placed in front of us Heidi caught the straw as she reached for a paper napkin and overturned the cup. Sticky caramel liquid and ice cubes ran all over the table and onto the floor. Then while reaching for more napkins she spilled one of the other drinks as well. This one spilled onto the seats occupied by Sully and me.

Heidi started to laugh and so did we but suddenly she began to cry. Heidi insisted on leaving even though Sully and I tried to minimize what had happened.

Sully agreed to ask the waitress to put our orders in a bag to take with us. I tried to give him money to pay for our food, but he refused. Sully told me he would bring the food out to my car if we would wait for him out there. I agreed.

Heidi and Mitch settled down in the car and we waited for Sully.

"Hank is going to be furious," Heidi cried.

"Honey, it was an accident. Anyone can have an accident. Besides, I think it was funny and I'm the one wearing wet britches," I joked.

Heidi didn't find it funny. She had noticed that someone from Hank's office was in the diner and she felt sure that he would tell Hank what happened. This reaction went beyond embarrassment, it was shame. She was afraid of what Hank's reaction would be to her public clumsiness. She began to cry again.

Sully brought out three small sacks and three drinks from the diner to the car about ten minutes later. He smiled a toothy genuine smile. So far I had seen Sully twice and he smiled most of the time.

"How're ya doin,' kid?" he directed to Heidi.

"I'm so sorry. I know I overreacted. It must be this pregnancy. I cry at the drop of a hat. Can't remember bein' this bad the first time," she stroked Mitch's head. He had been sitting on her lap.

Mitch was beginning to get restless and climbed over the back seat and onto the trunk of the car.

"Don't think nuthin' of it," Sully laughed, as he picked Mitch up and tickled him. He put Mitch down in the back seat.

"We need to get this child home for our nap, don't we, Mitch?" her tone hinted urgency.

We thanked Sully and said goodbye, then drove back to Heidi's place.

She seemed worn-out, and sad. "I really, really wanted to spend the day with you, Becka. I am just so dog-gone tired. I need to go up in and rest. I am so sorry."

Instead of being sent away, I insisted on staying and being there for Mitch when he woke up from his nap so that she could get as much sleep as she could. Heidi tried to refuse but it didn't work. She laid down on top of the bedcovers and fell quickly asleep, too tired to eat.

Mitch and I ate our sandwiches and he drank a glass of milk that I poured him. I hid the soda pop before he could see it. Afterward, Mitch fought hard to stay awake but sleep shortly overcame him, once I had laid him down in his small bed. Sitting beside him I stroked his back and soon he began softly snoring.

Mitch's room was within hearing distance of Heidi's room. I could hear her sniffing. She was awake and crying again.

I went into her room. "What's a matter, Shug?" I asked.

"Oh, Becka! I don't know," she sobbed.

I went over and sat on the bed beside her and held her close like we used to do as children when one of us was afraid or hurting. She held me tightly.

Once she sat back on the bed, I pushed her brown hair away from her face. She apologized again.

"You've been doing that all day. You don't have anything to apologize about. I'm your sister, remember?"

As little girls we made a pact to become 'blood sisters.' It was something we had seen in the movies when two men had become blood brothers. There was no actual blood shed between us, but the pact was, at least to us, a lifelong bond.

"Now, tell me. What has you so upset.?"

She hesitated, and then said "Really, Becka, I don't know. It's nothing big. Just a lot of little things, like today when I spilled the Cokes. I'm sure it will get back to Hank. That person, Buck, from his office was laughing. He thought it was funny. He'll tell Hank and Hank will act like he thinks its funny in front of everyone else, but when he gets home he'll be cross with me."

"There's nothing to be cross about. Anyone can have a little accident," I replied.

"I know, but lately I've been so clumsy. He married a woman with charm and grace. At least, that's what he thought.

Now he thinks I'm awkward and silly." There were still tears in her eyes.

"You? You are the most charming and graceful person I know. If you feel awkward at nine months pregnant it's BECAUSE you're nine months pregnant," my volume went up more than I intended and we heard Mitch stir. We looked toward the door and waited a moment. There was no further stirring from his room. "Sugar, you'll be back to your usual self soon. At my birthday party you were exceedingly gracious and charming."

"I made a pig outa myself," she cried.

I wondered if Hank had belittled her after they left the party. I remember him complaining about how much she was eating that day. Of course, she could have been critical of herself afterward. I couldn't know what was said between them.

"Did Hank say something to you about it?"

She looked down at the bed. "I don't think I realized how much I've been eating lately. I saw Dr. Stanton on Monday. He said I've gained more weight than he liked. Mama scolded me, too"

"You'll lose that after the baby comes. Don't worry so much about it. The thing is, are you eating healthy? Lots of fruits and vegetables?" I asked.

"Yes, but I've been craving sweets so much."

We talked about her diet and what food she should chose for hers and her baby's health now and after it is born. How much she was eating wasn't the only thing on her mind. That was only the tip of the iceberg.

She shared that Hank was more critical of everything she did than before they were first married. Heidi made excuses for his behavior. The wife of a lawyer must measure up to certain expectations. Some of the things she encountered were things to which she wasn't accustomed. Home must be perfect at all times, clean and tidy. Children were to be smart, respectful and clean. She was to belong to social clubs that her husband belonged to and participate in its activities like socials, fundraisers, and cocktail parties.

"Becka, I never had a cocktail in my life, until I married Hank. It took some getting used to. I still don't like the taste. How can people drink those things? Martinis? Yuck!"

She needed to hold her own in conversations about world affairs, current events and local issues. "I don't have time to sit down and read a newspaper. How am I sposed to keep up?"

My focus was on her drinking to fit in. I had been reading lately in medical journals about the negative effect of alcohol on infants.

"Did you tell Dr. Stanton that Hank wants you to drink? Did he say that it is alright?" I asked.

"I didn't think to mention it. Is it bad for the baby? I've known other women who had a cocktail now and then when they were pregnant and their babies were alright," she looked worried.

"I haven't read enough about it to give you advice, but I do think you should talk to him about it."

She agreed to ask Dr. Stanton and not drink with Hank until she had an OK from the doctor.

Heidi hadn't gone to college after high school. She felt inadequate when she was in the crowd with the lawyers and their wives. She was much younger than most of the wives and she couldn't tell me if any of them had attended college except two who bragged about it. But the others never mentioned anything. I told her that she might assume from their silence on the matter that they hadn't gone to college either or that they were more gracious than to boast about it. I advised her that she didn't have to share that information if no one asked. She said no one had asked. That seemed to make her feel a little better about it.

I hoped that the events of this day was just an issue with

fluctuating hormones causing her to be weepy and depressed, but then a seed was planted. Maybe Heidi was being emotionally manipulated and belittled by Hank. Mrs. Anderson seemed to be advocating that her daughter assume the role of obedient subservient wife. I was in hopes that she was at least emotionally supportive.

I stayed with Heidi until it was time for Hank to come home. We picked up Mitch's toys, got him washed up and prepared dinner together. She invited me to stay to dinner, but I made up an excuse. I really did not want to be there when Hank got home. My original impressions of Hank were being confirmed. She looked better before I left.

Later, I discussed my concerns with Papa. I came to my own conclusions which Papa confirmed. There was nothing I could do for Heidi other than be her friend, be there when she needed me, and pray for her. God and I were now on speaking terms. I prayed daily.

CHAPTER 16

Kids Again

Early on Friday morning, Papa rose and after his daily devotion time, left the house. Lorelei got busy cleaning the bathroom, and then moved on to clean the bedrooms. During the day I noticed that she rarely sat down and relaxed. Even her meals were eaten with urgency so that she could get on to the next chore. She worked too hard.

She was dusting the headboard after making the bed in Papa's room, when I stopped her to talk.

"Lorelei, I need to get you out of the house. We need to go do something fun," I proclaimed.

Certain she would resist, I tried to entice her with suggestions.

"We can pick up a bucket of fried chicken and have a picnic, or go to the Roller Rink and go skating. We can go for a ride or swim or…"

"Swim?" she reacted.

"Today is a beautiful day. It would be so refreshing to go swimming. How about it?" I giggled.

Lorelei just about squealed; she was so excited at the

thought of playing hooky from her self-imposed drudgery. "Where?"

She put away her rags and furniture polish.

"I've been missing that old swimming hole out past the pasture. Can we still get to it?" I inquired.

The wooded areas behind the pasture had overgrown with brush over the years. The creek ran through the back of Papa's property.

"I think we can get through the path. My old bathin' suit might just fall apart though. It might be dry-rotted for all I know," she seemed to be making excuses, but she was excited. From the way she walked out of the room so quickly putting away her work, I know she was delighted.

"Tell you what…I'll take you to Rose's Department store and we can pick you up a new suit," I matched her enthusiasm. She agreed and within fifteen minutes we jumped into my T-bird and sped down the road with the wind in our hair and sun warming our faces.

After an hour of agonizing comparison shopping, trying on the same three swim suits over and over, she made her choice. It was a royal blue one piece with skinny straps, white trim and a short flouncy skirt. The truth is she looked great in each one.

We did pick up a bucket of fried chicken and all the fixins and went back home to change into our bathing suits. We put half of the food in the Calvinator to be dinner for the family that night and took the rest for our picnic.

I put on my red checkered halter top bathing suit and gathered up some towels. It was just the two of us since Paul had gone out early to run errands for Mr. Anderson.

The path behind Papa's pasture had begun to grow over with various vegetation. Some of the wild blackberries seemed to reach out and grab our legs as we went through, causing little scratches. I made a mental note that we should wash them good with soap and water and apply some ointment when we got back to the house. Also, that if we do this again we could bring Papa's hedge shears with us.

"I didn't remember there were all these blackberry bushes back heya," Lorelei said as she handed me a handful of plump ripe berried that she had just picked. "There's so many heya. I could make some blackberry pie. I could put some jam up, too. Ooh, blackberry jam."

"Are we picking blackberries or going swimming? If we're going to pick berries I need to change clothes," I teased.

"I plan to come back later, Becka. I want to swim, too," she cooed.

We pushed our way through the path to the clearing. We could hear the water gurgling even before we saw it. Once we got to the clearing my heart raced a little bit. It was so beautiful. The grass ended about ten feet before the water's edge. The ground was covered with tiny smooth stones that were easy to walk on in bare feet and sloped gently to the shallow water. Off to the right was an old oak tree with a sturdy limb that jutted out far over the water. The rope that Papa had told Aaron to tie around that limb many years ago, when we were children, was still dangling over the water. After all these years the rope might not be good any more, I thought to myself, but was going to try it. The rope was for swinging out over the deep center of the creek and dropping into the water.

When I looked at Lorelei, she immediately guessed what I was thinking.

"You are not goin' to swing on that old thing are you?" she asked.

I couldn't help but smile with the widest smile, remembering the sensation of soaring up into the air and gliding momentarily before plunging into the cold water below. Aaron, Matt and I, and all the children we would invite took turns, everyone laughing and screaming and chattering with excitement. The boys would yodel like Tarzan.

The rope was positioned out on the limb far enough away that you couldn't just reach out from the water's edge. Papa wanted to make sure no one would drop into the shallow water and get hurt. I climbed up on the stump that shot up beside the big old oak tree and jumped out as far as I could to grab hold of the rope. It worked. The flying sensation was exhilarating. Lorelei was laughing and clapping from the bank of the creek. She came running into the water, splashing herself to acclimate to the cold. We played like children until we were hungry and then we threw an old tablecloth on the ground and spread out our feast. The food tasted astonishingly good.

"I have never seen you enjoy food so much, Becka, dear!" she commented.

"It's delicious," I confessed.

She joined in ravenously gobbling chicken and jojos, along with me. Lorelei wasn't one to be shy about eating. But no matter how much she indulged she never gained an ounce of weight.

After finishing our picnic, we laid down on our towels. I watched the leaves dance against the background of the azure sky. Life at that moment was so sublime.

Then Lorlelei broke the sweet silence

"Do you ever see that boy, Josh, up there? Does he still scare you?" her tone one of sincere concern.

The question took me aback. I couldn't imagine that she knew anything about Josh. I didn't think Papa would have shared my secret with her. Not sure where it came from, my first instinct was to deny that I knew what she was talking about.

"Scare me? What are you talking about?" almost immediately I tried to cut off her answer, "I mean, I don't ever see him. And I've never been scared of Josh," my answer sounded defensive.

"Of course you were, Becka. He molested you when you were a little girl. I could see even back then that he scared you," she was more apologetic than accusatory.

"You could? How did you know?" a million reasons she could have known ran through my mind. The worst reason imaginable would have been that he bragged about it to people. I asked "Did everyone know?"

My previous joy descended into dark fear.

"I don't think so, Becka. Aaron told me that he was sure that Josh had done something bad to you. He worried so about you."

"But it happened a long time before you and Aaron were going together," I said.

"We were goin' together a long time before anyone else knew 'bout us. I know you didn't know me, but I knew who you were. I could see such a change in you all at once. You had been so happy. I sort a envied you. I saw you laughin' and playin' with the other kids. Don't think I ever smiled until I met Aaron. Anyway, there was a change that even I could see," she explained.

"Mrs. Anderson thought I was just being sensitive because my mother had died and other girls had their mothers to teach them and do the things only mothers did with their daughters. I thought that seemed like a good excuse to me, so I let them think that was why I became so withdrawn."

She responded "I don't know what people thought or said. It wasn't until Aaron told me what happened that it made sense to me. He said that you never told him. He made Josh tell him," Lorelei said.

"Did Aaron ever say what he did to Josh? Because one day Josh just stopped looking for me? I saw him around for a while but he never spoke to me or even looked at me. I wondered why he stopped bothering me. I suspected Aaron had something to do with it," I said.

"He wanted to kill him. You know how bad his temper was. He told me that he followed Josh around for several days trying to catch him alone, but he was always with a mob of boys around him. Then one day he watched him sneak out of school and he followed him into the alley behind the movie theatre. Aaron grabbed a pipe that was on the ground just layin' there beside the garbage cans. He asked Josh what he had done to you. He told me Josh told him a bunch of lies about you but Aaron knew that Josh had molested you. He beat Josh with that pipe. He left him there to die but he didn't die. Aaron thought that he might go to prison for murder, so he was relieved and angry that he didn't kill Josh. Josh looked pretty bad for a couple of weeks when he came back to school. He threatened to get Aaron back but Aaron wasn't afraid of him. I don't think Aaron was afraid of anything in his life. Do you?" she asked.

She was still so in love with him all those years later.

"No. I don't think I ever saw him scared," I confirmed her need to believe him fearless. Aaron was only afraid of showing fear, I believed. "Well, to answer your question - am I afraid of Josh? No. I never see him. Cincinnati is a very big city. There's not much of a chance that I'll ever see him. If I did I wouldn't be afraid of him. You don't have to worry about me," I proclaimed falsely.

"You are just like Aaron, sometimes. More than you know," she declared.

We both got quiet again for a moment. I lay back down on my towel and looked at the sky again still feeling unsettled. Willa forgave Homer. As yet, even though Elaine had instructed me that was something I needed to do also, it had never entered my mind, until now. As I lay there unfocused on the leaves and sky Josh's face appeared in my mind. I could see his lewd smile and feel his rough hands. Could I ever forgive him? Feeling vulnerable and exposed laying there in my bathing suit, I began shaking violently. My teeth chattered. Just two days before I had turned it all over to God after Papa's sermon. Why couldn't I let it go? What was God's plan? If I forgave Josh, why was I still falling apart at the thought of him?

Talk about something else, I told myself to get my thoughts in another direction.

"Lor? Have you ever forgiven your father for what he did to you?" Immediately, I regretted asking the question. "I'm sorry. I have no right asking such a question."

"Actually, I was thinking about that on Wednesday, after Papa preached on forgiveness. He and I had talked about it many times over the years and I *did* turn it over to the Lord. If Papa could forgive the men who murdered his mother then I should be able to forgive my mama and daddy, right? But that day, I started thinking about my mama and daddy and I didn't feel sad or angry. Truth be told, I didn't feel anything but pity for them. The Lord had taken all of that away. Jesus said in Matthew *'love your enemies. Pray for those who hurt you.'* I prayed for mama and daddy a lot.

"When daddy died four years ago I went through it all over again. Way back, when Paul was a little feller, just starting school, I went to daddy's house to talk to him. For some reason, I had this outlandish notion that they might be regretting missing out on their grandson. I thought that if they could get to know him they would love him.

"Well when I got there, mama came running out of the front door with her broom in her hands threatening to hit me with it. I remember trying to introduce her to Paul and she said 'don't you call him my grandson' then she called him a *'stinking indian'* and she called me a *'harlot.'* Daddy came out, too. I told him that I forgave him, but that made him mad. They chased us away. I cried but not because of what they said. I know better, Becka. I cried for them. They didn't want to know Paul. They missed out on all the love he had to offer.

"So when daddy died, I hurt all over again because he rejected Paul. But, Becka, Paul and me have been so well loved by Papa, you, Benji, Matt, and Ginny, and the whole church family that I know I never missed out. Most of all, the Lord took care of us through everyone He put in our lives.

"But once in a while, now please don't be cross with me, but once in a while I get angry with Aaron for leaving us. And I know that doesn't make any sense. He got killed. He didn't choose to get killed, but selfishly, I wanted more of him. I still miss him," she got quiet for a moment. Her voice was clear and strong. She did not get choked up or tearful. "Even with all the love surrounding me, I sometimes feel sorry for myself. But it doesn't last very long."

"I could never be cross with you, Lor," I turned to look at her, then out of nowhere came a question I had no right to ask . "Did your daddy molest you?"

She looked shocked. "Molest? You mean…? Oh, No. No. My Daddy? No."

"I'm sorry. I shouldn't have asked. It's just that I had a case in the hospital last month. There was this young girl, twelve years old, and her father, well actually her step-father…" I stammered out of embarrassment. "He raped her repeatedly over a few years and then he beat her so badly that she almost died. She's been on my mind so much."

"Oh, Lawd! How awful. Is she alright?" she sat upright.

"She seems to be doing well. She was discharged and went home with her mother. Her step-father will be sitting in jail for a long time for it."

"Well, I hope so," she snapped. Indignant. "My daddy never, never…That poor child."

"You know, Lor, it's perfectly normal to be angry with someone who had died," I was thinking of what she said about Aaron. "People are afraid to tell others because they think they are bad people for having those feelings but a lot of people do. You are not a bad person for having them," I reassured her.

"Have you ever felt that way?" she asked me for validation.

"I don't know. I've gotten good at stuffing my feelings way down deep so I don't have to deal with them but I have a friend who has been telling me that by doing that I am hurting myself. She may be right," I said as I took inventory of my feelings. The shaking had stopped. "I don't want to talk about this anymore. Let's talk about something else. Something fun," I requested.

"OK, what?" she flipped onto her belly and pulled her feet up behind her.

"Tell me about Mr. Sullivan."

"Oh, now I want to change the subject," she blushed.

"He seems like a real nice fella. And I think he really likes you. Has he asked you to go out with him? He's young to have his own business. He could own half the town one day," I teased.

"Mr. Anderson owns one half and The Owens' own the other half. There are no more halves to be owned," she teased back.

Lorelei admitted that she liked Sully but only said that she was worried about leaving Papa alone if she were to consider a serious relationship. Even though I tried to convince her that Papa would be ok, what she said hadn't been anything I had taken into consideration before. How would Papa manage alone in that big house if all his children were gone?

She also spoke about being "unequally yoked" which was a reference to Sully's not being a believer. A Christian who married a non-believer was in an uphill battle from the start.

"Papa seems to like him; maybe he feels Sully is close to accepting Jesus. The way he teased you on the way home from the cemetery I got the impression he might like to see you two together," I asserted.

She responded "He told me that I should go out with Sully. I think you're right. I think he thinks he can convert him. But I wouldn't know how to act on a date. Anyway, I've been praying about it. I really have been praying that he will start coming to church. If the Lord brings him to church I might just have to start going out with him."

I was beginning to feel more relaxed. We talked for at least another hour about lighter things. With dinner already planned for that evening Lorelei was able to relax and enjoy an entire day off. I swam a little more before we set off back to the house. We knew that the next day was going to be a somber one.

CHAPTER 17
Jasper Jenkins

Mr. Jenkins's funeral was well attended. He had been liked by everyone. While he only had one remaining daughter, Suri, he had ten grandchildren, thirty-one great grandchildren, and many great-great grandchildren, brothers, sisters, nieces and nephews. I did not know that Mr. and Mrs. Jenkins had lost three children during the influenza outbreak in 1917. I found this out when Dr. Stanton delivered the eulogy for Mr Jenkins.

He had been a fireman, a councilman, and even was Mayor for a term before his wife became ill and he and Suri had to care for her.

Mrs. Stanton was a close friend of Mrs. Jenkins who had welcomed her to Belmont and taken her under her wing and nurtured her when the doctor and his wife were strangers in a new place. Mrs. Stanton had helped Mr. Jenkins and Suri take care of Mrs. Jenkins when she became confused and dependent.

The funeral, while sad, was a lovely salute to a life well lived. His grandchildren and great-grandchildren performed music that Mr. Jenkins loved. They played Bluegrass Gospel songs like "Softly and Tenderly Jesus is Calling" and "What A Friend We Have In Jesus" and more. It seemed to me that as I was growing up there was music everywhere. Our family and friends got together so often at our place that I took it for granted. When we visited friends at their homes there were always musicians playing banjos, fiddles, guitars, mandolins, or dulcimers. Music was such a part of all of us.

His family, though were known throughout the area as gospel singers and performed at churches and gatherings throughout the county.

After the funeral and the graveside service, friends and family were invited back to the Jenkins's home to spend time together. Tables of food were set up on the grass beside the house, but the morning sky was bleak with gray clouds, threatening rain. So the tables were moved into the house and on the porch.

I saw a group of friends sitting, talking on the front porch and so I went up to visit. Nancy and Letha, two of his granddaughters, were cousins, close to my age. We had gone to school, church, and Sunday school together. They wore black like most of the family.

"Hey, Becka. Come over and take a look at this," Nancy said. She was holding a large photo album.

"Look," she said pointing to a picture of Mr. Jenkins lifting me into his airplane. I was, maybe, seven or eight years old. A picture just below it showed the two of us sitting in that plane with our goggles on, mine covered most of my face. "That's you!" Letha said.

Mr. Jenkins had a pilot's license and owned a red biplane with an open cockpit. Sometimes he would take us children up for rides in his airplane.

"Those airplane rides were so much fun," I stated.

"They were," Nancy agreed.

I had never been on a commercial flight but I couldn't have imagined that they would have been any more wonderful than riding in Mr. Jenkins' 1947 Stearman biplane. In his plane, I felt the wind on my face, and saw the trees and streams, the fields and buildings below in full view. Sometimes, if he flew through a low cloud there was a sensation of dew dampening my skin.

"Whatever happened to that old plane?" George popped up behind me.

"It's in that old hanger in the back of the property. It's a mess; all rusty and paint peeling. Mice have the seats all tore up. Grandpa would have been so sad to see it in this shape. He hadn't been back there in years. But before he got sick he still went back and cranked the engine up and washed the hull. The runway is all overgrown now, too. Can't say he loved it more than us, but it might have been a close race," Nancy said.

George took my hand casually as if I wouldn't notice. It was reassuring. I moved closer to him.

"Mr. Jenkins took me up a couple of times, too. Did he ever do rolls when you were up there with him?" George directed the question to everyone.

"I think he knew better than to do that with me in there. I would have vomited," Nancy said.

"Me either, did he roll it with you?" Letha asked Tommy, another cousin.

"No. He kept it pretty level," Tommy said.

Other cousins also said that he never rolled the plane with them in it. George said, "He did with me. I nearly threw up."

I was the only one beside George in that group that Mr. Jenkins rolled the plane while they were riding in it. "I loved it," I said.

Nancy said, "Grandpa said that he liked to take you up, Becka. He said that you weren't scared of anything. He said that you could have been the wing-walker to his barnstorm, or better yet he said that you should learn to fly yourself."

"Funny. Not scared of anything. Good Lord, I was scared of everything, except flying in that airplane. But I knew Mr. Jenkins wouldn't let anything happen to me up there in the air. I don't know if I would ever even think of walking out on the wing, though," I remarked.

We knew the story of Mr. Jenkins and his history of flying. In World War I he learned to fly a Niueport II, a type of airplane used in dogfighting. He knew Eddie Rickenbacker. Mr. Jenkins didn't have as many dogfights as the Ace, Rickenbacker, but he had shot down many enemy planes. His plane never went down and he had quite a few medals from the war.

Mr. Jenkins didn't know Papa or Dr. Stanton during the war but when they got together they talked quite a bit about England and France, about comrades in arms and pretty girls they met there. Mr. Jenkins was already married when he went over there, but he would say "No harm done in admiring the scenery." He was charming and good looking, so he might have broken a few hearts.

George wanted to take a walk back to see the old plane. I did not want to see it. It would have broken my heart to see that beautiful old thing decaying and neglected. Thankfully the sky opened up and thunder made us all jump just as it started to downpour. No trip to the hanger.

From that time on, however, I began to dream of learning to fly. I thought that maybe somewhere in Ohio I could find someone who could teach me. I would begin checking on it when I went back.

Later that day, I finally got to spend some more time alone with Papa. The rain cleared up and the clouds gave way to sunshine so we walked back to the old swimming hole. We just sat and talked for hours.

CHAPTER 18

The Baby Comes

George was a persistent visitor. He came to see me every day. After missing me on Thursday when I visited Heidi and again on Friday when I visited Lorelei, he began to make 'appointments' with me. I had to beg off a few days because I wanted to have Papa to myself.

Unlike when we were adolescents, no one chaperoned us when we went out, although George told me that his mother felt that we should be supervised. That seemed silly to me. I was nearly thirty years old and had been living on my own now for ten years with college, medical school, internship and residency. George had lived on his own even longer. Together we went to visit Heidi on Tuesday. George shared my concern about his sister's health. She was still tired and depressed. Her ankles were extraordinarily swollen. I told her that she must get in to see Dr. Stanton right away. At my insistence she called him and made an appointment for that afternoon. George and I took her and Mitch to that appointment.

Heidi's blood pressure was dangerously high. Dr. Stanton decided that she should be admitted to the hospital at that time. George drove us all to the hospital. Hank and Mr. and Mrs. Anderson came to the hospital as soon as George called them to tell them what was going on.

She began having convulsions after she was admitted. Her condition is known as eclampsia and could have been fatal to both Heidi and her baby. Dr. Stanton immediately consulted with an obstetrician and began giving her IV medications to control the seizures. They would need to deliver the baby as soon as she was stable.

I called Papa from the hospital to let him know. Mrs. Anderson contacted almost every lady from church and started a prayer chain. Papa arrived about the time that Heidi was going in to the delivery room to have a cesarean section. He prayed with the family. We stayed all evening until the doctor came out to tell us about the condition of mother and child.

A little girl was born weighing five pounds, two ounces. She was about four weeks early and was what was known as a 'blue baby' because she had been deprived of oxygen and her skin had a bluish tint. Heidi was doing well but was sedated. She wouldn't be told about her baby until the next day.

Hank was distraught. He had never even thought about a possibility that their child could have something wrong with it. "What does that mean? Blue Baby? Will it die?" he couldn't bring himself to call her 'she,' only 'it.'

"I will be honest, Hank," Dr. Stanton said, "It is possible that she may not make it. She is early and very, very small. She went through a lot to come into this world. We will keep her warm, and give her oxygen.

"I need to go outside," Hank told the doctor. He looked pale and shaky.

Papa said kindly "I'll come with you, Hank. Let's get you some water or something."

"No," Hank snapped, and then took a deep breath before he spoke again. "I'm going to go down the street for a drink."

Mrs. Anderson argued with him that Heidi would need him when she woke up. But he paid her no attention as he walked down the hall and through the door to the elevator.

After Dr. Stanton and the obstetrical doctor left the area, Mrs. Anderson began asking me questions about their new grandchild. I told her all the possible scenarios that could result from the traumatic birth from severe mental retardation to mild mental impairment, from needing total custodial care all her life to simple delay in walking and talking but with the ability to perform self-care.

"Some of these children are able to hold jobs and live on their own. Only time will tell. Heidi should be alright now. She should be out of danger. But she will need as much support as we can give her. Hank will need time, too," I said, but what I was thinking was very different. He was expecting a perfect life with a perfect family and this would change everything.

Shortly afterward, the doctor allowed us to go in to see the baby through the nursery window. She was beautiful even with her pale bluish complexion. She lay still under a little oxygen tent. Mrs. Anderson commented on her perfectly shaped head.

"Often with cesarean sections, they are like that," I told them.

With every little stir she made, grandma and grandpa ooh'd and ahh'd in amazement. Little Mitch, too was in awe.

"Is that my new little sister?" he asked as George lifted him up so he could look through the window.

"Yes, Mitchy, now you're the big brother and you'll have to protect your little baby sister," Grandpa Anderson told him.

"She looks like a baby doll," he beamed. He saw no imperfection in her.

We waited for hours for Hank to return but he did not. After a while Mr. Anderson said "I'm going to find him and drag his butt back here. He should be here for my little girl and my granddaughter."

"Dad, let me go," George stepped in. He knew that his father was angry and seemed to know that a confrontation wouldn't go well.

Although I would have liked to stay for Heidi and be there when she woke up, I told Mrs. Anderson that I could take Mitch home and stay with him for the night. He was getting restless and tired. Also, he didn't need to see his father in whatever condition that he might return, nor be frightened by harsh words that could be exchanged. She thanked me. And I asked Papa to drive me to Heidi's house so I could put Mitch to bed.

George, Papa, Mitch, and I walked out of the hospital together. As we separated in front of the hospital, I kissed George on the cheek. It was just a quick peck, but he stopped and said "See that wasn't so hard was it?" and laughed. It was impulsive and I hadn't even thought about it. I laughed as well.

The next day was Wednesday and I was expected to return to Cincinnati Children's Hospital on the following Monday morning. This caused me no little concern. My best friend needed me but being newly hired I didn't want to disappoint the hospital and Dr. Spence.

"How much time do you think you will need, Doctor Aldridge?" Dr. Spence sounded irritated over the telephone.

It was a question that I had anticipated but wasn't sure of the answer. It could be months before Heidi and the baby would be in the clear. Of course, the hospital would never grant me that much time. So I considered what would be a reasonable length of time to request. I would ask for two more weeks.

Dr. Spence took my request to the board and called me back the next morning on Heidi's telephone. The board rejected the request. They expected me to return as originally agreed on Monday morning. I thanked him for taking it to the board and told him that I would be there on Monday morning.

My original plan was to start my drive home on Friday morning so that I could have the entire week end to rest. Plans changed to allow me to start my drive home early on Sunday morning. This would give me only two additional days in Belmont.

Before lunchtime on Wednesday, Wilma Fauntleroy and Roy came by Heidi's place to take care of Mitch. She asked me question after question about Heidi and the baby while the two boys played in Mitch's playroom. Hearing the concern in Wilma's voice I offered to watch both boys so that she could go and see Heidi for herself. But she said, "No, you should go. I'll be right here when she comes home. You should spend the time with her while you can. I know you'd stay if you could."

Papa called to see if I needed a ride to back to the hospital, but George had arrived only minutes before to pick me up. He hugged his nephew while I collected a few things on a list that Mrs. Anderson had given to him to bring for Heidi.

George had sold his car before he went off to do missionary work. He borrowed one of his father's company's old pick-up trucks whenever he came back home. The old Chevy truck was dirty and rusty and made a lot of noise. George kept the windows down because the exhaust smell was awful. The springs were shot and every bump in the road jolted the spine. But George had spread one of his mother's clean sheets over the bench seat so that I would not get my dress dirty. I thought about asking him to take me back to Papa's house so I could change clothes and drive my own car but I didn't want to be rude.

"How long did you stay at the hospital last night?" I asked him.

"We stayed all night. I just got home a little while ago to

shower and change clothes," he said. It must have dawned on him at that moment that I was wearing the same dress I had on the day before. He pulled into a gas station parking lot and turned around to go back. "I should have taken you home first. I'm sorry, Becka."

"Don't turn around, George. We are half way there now. It's alright. Just keep going," I urged. He was very tired and worried about his sister.

"Did Hank come back last night?" I asked him.

"No. I looked for him half the night but couldn't find him."

"Was Heidi awake this morning? Does she know about the baby?" I asked.

"Yes."

"How are they both doing?"

He sighed "She's crying and upset. The baby isn't crying which is upsetting. She's not eating. Babies have to eat pretty soon after they're born, right?"

"She'll eat, George. They may have to put a tiny little tube down her nose to her stomach for a while to feed her, but they won't let her starve. It just might take her some time to learn to suck. She won't starve," I reassured him.

"It's good that you know so much about babies," he said matter-of-factly.

"I guess I had better since that's what I went to school for all this time," I said just as matter-of-factly.

He was quiet for a long time. Our clothes smelled like exhaust fumes.

"George? When Benji was born, no one knew what his life would like. It was pretty good. Everyone loved him. He loved everyone. The only thing he had to worry about was if he would get bananas for breakfast or cake for dessert, or if Papa would sing him to sleep at night. With all the love this baby's going to get she'll have a good life," I told him.

"Somehow, I don't see her daddy singing her to sleep," he

said bitterly. He was very angry with Hank. "He had better be there when we get there."

Our silence again filled the truck, but the clanking of metal, squeaking of springs, traffic and road noise was extremely loud.

Then he asked "How long did it take *your* father to accept Benji? I bet he didn't have to think about it."

"Well, since Mama died, I guess he didn't have a choice. I think Hank will come around. He was expecting a perfect child. She is still *his* child. And once he sees how cute she is he won't be able to help falling in love with her. She is beautiful, isn't she?"

"She is," he agreed.

Studying George, a proud uncle and loving brother, it seemed as if I had never really seen him before. He sat tall behind the steering wheel of that old truck, thoughtful. There was a slight upturn in the corner of his mouth pushing the dimple in his clean shaven cheek deeper. His red hair was beginning to grow slightly over his ears and collar. It was longer than he usually kept it. Likely he would be getting a haircut soon.

I knew him and at the same time I didn't. He was thinking about Heidi. He was thinking about Hank and the baby. Was he thinking about me?

"Heidi didn't say they had a name in mind when we visited. Did they ever mention one to you?"

"Henry, like his daddy or Henrietta, I suppose."

I crinkled my nose without intending to make a face. George must have glanced my way at the time I did it.

"Yeah. That's what I think, too," he said.

"No. It's not bad. Old fashioned, but pretty. Mitch is going to be a terrific brother to little Henrietta," I offered my opinion.

George's smile grew wider, his dimple deeper.

"Just like you. You're a wonderful brother to Heidi," I added.

"She's a good kid," he paused for a moment before continuing. "Hank isn't around very much for them. Our dad, even though he had his businesses, he was there for us. Dad was at all my basketball games, our high school programs and plays. You make time for what's important to you."

"What do you mean, George?" I asked.

"Hank worships something else. His time is spent working and hardly ever with his family. He goes to church but I don't think that his heart is right with God."

"Why do you think that?" I asked.

"Hank is busy trying to impress other lawyers, businessmen and judges rather than spend time with Heidi and Mitch. It's one thing to do lawyer work whatever that is, but something else to go off drinking and golfing, and just staying out all night when he has a family at home waiting for him," George was clearly getting agitated.

"Heidi has never said anything about any of that to me. Hank doesn't come home at night?" My initial reaction had been to defend him. He might be trying to create contacts that would help his firm by golfing even getting a drink with a client or associate. Professionals needed to link up with other professionals to build their clientele, but not coming home at night wasn't part of a business attorney's obligation. I just left it at the question.

"She doesn't say anything to me, either. My Dad knows what goes on. He knows everyone in town and they all get back to him. It used to be tough as a kid trying to get away with anything. Everything gets back to him.

"Hank can be, really, I don't know. What would you call it? Charming? He swept Heidi off of her feet. Her 'Prince Charming.' You were her maid of honor. I'm sure she talked your ear off about him. She is still like that. Hank can do no wrong as far as Heidi is concerned," he continued, "I shouldn't say he isn't right with God. Only God knows someone's heart. Maybe he's like all other 'Yankees'. Be careful you don't turn into one yourself," George joked; his demeanor changing.

"What? A Yankee? Don't think there's a chance. I'm a southern gal. Don't really fit in up there. But I love what I'm doing," I told him.

"Do you get lonely up there?" he asked softly, thoughtfully.

"I've made some friends recently. Now that I am out of residency, I have some time to meet people and socialize a little bit. But like I said, I don't feel like I fit in. A lot of the folks I went to school with had the idea that people from the south were all hillbillies. I couldn't tell if they thought I'm stupid because I am from North Carolina or because I am a woman, but they treat me like I'm stupid. It doesn't offend me too much, George. I know I am intelligent. The one's that know me know that," I said as we arrived at the hospital.

We pulled into the parking spot and George got out and came around to open my door. He pulled the little light blue suitcase out of the back of the truck for Heidi and carried it in. With his free hand, George took my hand as we walked in through the doors. His hands were strong and slightly rough but his grasp was gentle.

Hank was at Heidi's bedside when we arrived. Mr. and Mrs. Anderson were sitting in chairs in her room. There were two beds in the room and the other bed was empty. There had only been five babies in the nursery the night before but I knew that could change very quickly. Babies had their own timing when coming into the world.

Heidi's eyes were red and her face splotchy from crying. She smiled when we came into the room.

"I am so glad you're here," she told both of us. "How's my little boy?" she asked.

"He had a good night. I left him playing with Roy. Wilma

is there with him," I smiled and reached over and kissed her cheek. She grabbed my hand.

"Have you seen her?" she asked. I knew she was asking about the baby.

"We saw her last night. Did you get to see her?" I asked.

"They haven't let me get out of bed yet. I'm just dyin' layin' here. I want to see my baby," she sniffed. She was sitting up in bed looking small and vulnerable. "They can't bring her to me because she is in the incubator. I'm about to go out of my mind, Becka," she nearly pleaded.

"Well let me go talk to the nurse. Has the doctor been in yet?"

"Not yet," Mrs. Anderson answered for her. "The curtains are closed in the nursery window. Why do you think they did that?" she asked.

"They usually only open the curtains during certain visiting hours. They don't want the babies on display all the time. I don't understand it, either, but most places are like that. Nurses are trying to feed the infants if the mothers can't for any reason, or they are changing them. They try to keep it quiet because if one starts crying many times they all start crying. It's better for the babies to have a quiet environment," I tried to sound knowledgeable but I didn't really know the reason. I suspected it was because the nurses didn't want to be on display or bothered by curious people tapping on the glass all the time.

"Speaking of feeding them…she should be getting some nutrition by now," Mrs. Anderson said.

Hank sat quietly beside Heidi, keeping his attention on her.

"What time did you get here, Hank? I looked for you until 3 in the morning," George demanded.

I was wishing that I had left to find the doctor when this came up.

Hank didn't answer. Heidi put her hand on his head and said "I'm sorry you were worried, George. It's alright now."

George let it go. Mr. Anderson didn't say anything. It was likely that much had already been said when Hank came back. There was no need to discuss it further in front of me.

"So, George told me you want to name her Henrietta," I stated.

Heidi laughed. "Oh, Lord, NO," it was good to see her laugh. "George was pulling your leg. We never said that. Her name is Lillian. She's my Li'l girl. I'm gunna call her Lil or Lily. Don't you love it?"

"Suits her. She is beautiful, Heidi. Hank, have you seen her?" I asked him.

Hank shook his head without looking away from Heidi.

"I'm going to go find the doctor, like I said. You *are* going to see your new baby girl this morning."

There are some extraordinary benefits to being an M.D. A few rules were bent and Heidi was helped into a wheelchair and she and Hank were permitted to go see their little girl. She was less blue than the night before and her cry was a little stronger but still weak. As I had explained to them, a small catheter had been placed down her nose to her stomach in order to give her formula.

Hank looked relieved to see his child looking 'normal.' He had convinced himself that she would be somehow disfigured. "Little Lily," he said his speech slightly slurred. He was quiet because he was hung-over. Hank's eyes were bloodshot and he had a day's growth of beard and his shirt and pants were wrinkled.

After his visit, he reluctantly agreed to come with me to get some coffee in the cafeteria. George and Mr. Anderson started off with us, but I discretely asked them to let me talk to him alone and they agreed.

"Rough night?" I started.

"You might say that," his only response.

"Heidi will be alright."

"Yeah, but what about the baby?" his question sounded near desperation

"She's not out of the woods, but she is in good hands. Are you afraid she's not going to make it?" I asked.

"Maybe afraid that she will," his honesty was unexpected. George had been right about Hank's 'Yankee' way.

"What worries you about her making it?" I said trying not to sound judgmental. I had made mistakes with Mrs. Lockhart in making judgments before I had all the facts. Hank needed to tell me. I was not going to guess what he was feeling.

"What do you mean? You said she could be retarded." The word made me cringe, but I kept quiet. "She might be a cripple. Someone might have to take care of her all of her life. What kind of a life is that?"

I took a breath and stayed calm. Was he really telling me about her life or the kind of life he feared for himself?

"First, Hank, I never used the word 'retarded.' If she has a mental disability that doesn't mean she can't hear, or understand, or think. She might need a champion from people who take for granted that she can't do any of those things. Whatever the outcome, expect the best for her. Make sure everyone treats her as a human being," I did not scold. Elaine had taught me more about communication by modeling it than I had ever learned in college.

Hank handed me a cup of coffee from the vending machine. It was barely drinkable but it was strong and just what Hank needed.

"Mental disability," he repeated.

"Did you know I had a little brother that was born with Cerebral Palsy? His name was Benji. He couldn't speak, but he could show love like nobody else. He loved everybody."

Hank interrupted me "Did he have a 'mental disability?'" spitting out the words mental disability with disgust.

"Yes. He is why I became a doctor. He saved my Papa's life."

"Huh?"

"After Mama died, I think Papa could have easily given up on life. But Benji needed him. Taking care of Benji gave Papa a renewed purpose in life. Benji brought a lot of happiness to people. Anyone who gave him a chance could see that he had a purpose, and that was to bring joy to people. His laugh could make anyone smile. He knew what was going on with people. Whenever anyone was sad, he got this concerned expression and did his best to cheer them up. Even if people treated him badly, he never got angry with them."

"A dog could do that," he replied. Now he was beginning to make me angry so I veered away from talking about Benji. The topic was too sensitive to me.

"Please don't let your mind go there. You can't think of people that way. Benji wasn't an animal and neither is Lily. She is a beautiful baby girl. I can see you in her eyes." Hank needed to be directed to think of his daughter as his, otherwise he would be able to distance himself from her.

He sipped his coffee noisily.

"Your family is going to need your attention."

"My job is demanding. I have to be in the office long days, sometimes late into the night. We can't let cases pile up. There are court deadlines. Clients expect me to do my job. They don't care if I have problems at home," he said defensively.

"I'm not in your place. Please don't think I am trying to criticize you. Your job is important. Your family is important, too. Somehow, you should find a way to balance all of that. I can't tell you how. My father would tell you that through prayer God can help you handle it."

He lowered his head. "Thanks," he said uncharacteristically humble. "I love my family. I do! Heidi's families don't think I do, but I do."

Hank had a lot to think about and unfortunately he had made a bad choice the night before and wasn't feeling very well. Mr. Anderson and George had given him a hard time and would continue to give him a hard time. I just hoped that he would be able to handle the challenges ahead of him.

We found out that Heidi wasn't going to be discharged for at least another week which meant that she wouldn't be home before I had to leave. Her family and friends were going to be able to give her more help than I could but I was sad that I couldn't be there for her.

I visited every day for hours each time. Little Lily was getting stronger with her tube feeding. No further complications had shown themselves in those few days and her chances of survival were getting better with each day. She would be in the hospital for quite some time after Heidi went home.

Hank went home every night to be with his son. Several of Heidi's friends took turns watching Mitch during the day and cleaning her house. Ladies from the church brought Hank and Mitch food every day and I was certain this would continue long after Heidi got to go home.

The most disappointing part was that I didn't get to spend as much time with Papa was I would have liked. I spent a little time with him every morning and every night, but cherished the time we did get to talk and pray together.

Sunday morning I packed my suitcases and returned home to Cincinnati.

CHAPTER 19
Return to Cincinnati

Dr. Spence welcomed me back in his cordial way on Monday morning. There was no indication of disappointment that I had requested additional time away.

It was an honor to have been chosen to receive the Fellowship out of what turned out to be dozens of applicants across the country. The next few months were very busy with research for Dr. Sabin's oral polio vaccine, as well as fulfilling an obligation to cover the Emergency Room one Saturday per month and searching for a practicing physician with which to partner.

I spoke with Heidi or her mother nearly every day by telephone. Usually the calls were short, but certain cues she gave, let me know when we needed to talk longer. If Heidi told me "Lily hasn't gained any weight." Or "Lily hasn't turned over yet" spoke of her concern for the baby's development. A few times she led the conversation with "Hank didn't come home last night." Those were the longer conversations.

George extended his visit home and returned to Africa in September. We spoke often by telephone before he left as well, but once he left the Trans-Atlantic calls were simply too costly and prohibitive. We wrote letters more often than we had before. To my surprise, I missed him more than I ever before.

Interviews with Dr. Nikola Nastasic in September lead to an offer to join his practice. It was an excellent opportunity to start building my own client base. Things were moving quickly.

Dr. Nastasik had come to America from Russia during the War. He spoke English fairly well and his patients found him easy to understand. This made a difference in establishing his practice. After the War Americans were suspicious of 'foreign' doctors and reluctant to go to them for treatment and if one had a thick accent it was much more difficult for them to trust that doctor.

Dr. Nastasic was ruggedly handsome and had a broad white toothy smile. He had a tendency to push his blond hair back with his left hand if he felt that one stray hair crept forward. In truth, his hair was perfectly obedient and stayed combed in place. He was five foot, six inches tall and a well-built 160 pounds. Whether in the office or at the hospital he wore his white hip length belted lab coat over his long sleeve shirt.

His office was a mile and a half away from the hospital. We shared exam rooms and office staff and for a while I would help him with his patients while I built up my own practice. Dr. Nastasic had office hours six days a week of which we shared four days and so each of us had one day alone in the office and a few days off. We made house calls as did many physicians in those days. In addition to seeing patients in the hospital and the office and one day a week working research, I would continue to work one day per month in the ER. Altogether, I worked five days a week and once a month spent time in the ER as well. Hospital time included performing some surgery such as tonsillectomies and appendectomies but pediatric surgeons did the more complex procedures.

Mrs. Nastasic, like her husband emigrated from Russia. Her English was not very good but she made it clear that she did not like me.

"Dr. Nastasic is married to me. You stay out of bed," she warned, her face inches from mine. Mrs. was full figured with dyed black hair and red lipstick. She was tiny and fierce. She couldn't imagine that I wouldn't be attracted to Dr. Nastasic. I was not. He was all business and not flirtatious with me nor anyone else that I had witnessed. She had nothing to worry about. He was devoted only to her and to medicine.

No friendship was likely to develop between Mrs. Nastasic and myself.

Elaine and I caught up at once upon my return from North Carolina.

"You look so refreshed, Becka," Elaine told me as we talked through the zoo, past the animals. "The trip must have done you much good."

"Many things got cleared up, but some things I am even more confused about," I stopped as I fed some peanuts to the elephants through the bars. "My father is so loving. I told you that I was angry at him and that the reason was ridiculous. He was not to blame for what happened to me, and that he didn't even know…"

"I remember. But from a child's perspective it sort of made sense, but you carried it into adulthood. Were you able to let it go?" she asked.

"I told him everything and asked him to forgive me. He apologized to ME. There was no reason to apologize to me. He cried with me because he felt he had let me down. Papa has very often taught all of us about forgiveness and he reminded me why it means so much.

"Elaine, I am praying every day. Sometimes, many times a day. I'm reading my Bible. Papa used to read to us out of the Bible all of the time, but I never did much on my own. We had to memorize scripture passages for Sunday school sometimes. There is a lot of comfort in there. There is a lot of distress, too. I mean punishment, admonishment, and wrath. I may be calling on you to help me understand some of what I read. Is that alright?" I asked.

"Of course, if I understand. I believe our Bibles may be a little different. I depend a great deal on our priest to teach from it. But as long as you are reaching out to the Lord, He will give you understanding," she encouraged me in this way.

I told her all about Heidi and the baby and she added them to her daily prayer list.

Then I talked to her about George. This was the part that, I admitted I was more confused about than before. For the first time, I was beginning to think I could have a future with George, even though he was half way around the world and I was newly established in Cincinnati with a new home and job.

"If it is ordained it will be," she said. This was less reassuring than her other encouragements. It was likely a topic she was less comfortable with as she was called to a life of celibacy. But she listened thoughtfully, but that conversation didn't go much further.

Between the hospital research fellowship and earnings from the practice, my salary was $6500.00 a year and would grow as my practice grew. Because of that, I found an adorable house that was up for rent just outside the city. It was a three story lap sided house with a turret on the front corner, three large bedrooms, a study and a large open kitchen like Papa's house. Three bedrooms and a large kitchen was more than I was likely to use, but family and friends whom I hoped would come to visit would have a comfortable place to stay.

The round turret room on the first floor was surrounded with three floor-to-ceiling windows. I made plans for a large Christmas tree to be set up in that room that would be seen by passers-by on the street. The second floor round room made a unique office/study. The home was lovely and within my budget.

A walkway came up from the sidewalk through a gated cast iron picket fence with spear and ball tops to a porch the entire length of the front of the house. Short hedges lined the inside of the fence and flowers were planted along the walkway. The swing that hung on the front porch was a perfect touch to remind me of Papa's house.

There was a driveway to the right of the house and a garage around the back at the end of the driveway. The garage was dark and had a damp feel to it. From the kitchen, the back door opened to stone cut steps that were even and flat, flanked by boxwood hedges and rows of flowers. In the back of the property, the fence went all the way around and separated it from neighbors whose back yard butted against mine. In front of the fence were a few fruit trees. There was a large apple tree, two cherry trees and a pear tree. I wasn't sure if I would ever have time to get out and tend to those flowers and trees or pick any of the fruit but it was lovely and fragrant. Maybe in time I could hire gardener to tend to these.

It was a perfect place to play hostess to friends. Elaine continued to join me once a week and I also went to the House with the Sisters once or twice a month. Sophie joined us as often as she could.

CHAPTER 20

Mrs. Hornsby

The idea of learning to fly continued to pester me, and was more urgent since my friend was struggling back home with her new baby. I imagined that I might be able to fly back home anytime I wanted and I began to make inquiries and thought that it was something I could make time to do. Harrison Airport was fifteen miles northwest of Cincinnati and there were flight instructors there who would teach using their own airplanes. Lessons were affordable but the cost of an airplane was out of the question at that time. Owning an airplane might have to wait for quite some time, and so would quick week-end trips back home. As things seemed to settle down back home and I became immersed in my medical practice and research, the urge to pursue flying took a back seat.

Heart-warming visits with Willa and her family and Mrs. Hornsby gave us all hope for friendship and a future. Whether at my home or the Sister's House the fellowship was dear to us all. The Sisters played games with the children and we continued to play our instruments but now we included Jerry who was learning to play the trumpet. Willa's voice was an amazing gift that she shared with all; unafraid and strong. One could lose themselves in the beauty of such a voice. Encouraged by her teachers, she blossomed when she was permitted to share her gift with others. Willa sang at recitals at school and solos at her church.

She invited me to come to her church on one of these visits to hear her perform. A few weeks later I took her up on the offer. Willa sang several solo songs during each service that I attended. Her gift was clear, perfect pitch each time without waiver. I had certainly heard some excellent performers in my life but these were professionally trained mature people while Willa was a beginner. She was taking lessons from a voice teacher that Mrs. Hornsby had secured for her.

The Assembly of God church differed from my father's church in that it was more reserved and the music more conservative and traditional. The people were just as warm and welcoming, often stopping to talk as if they had known me for years. Pastor Michael Hasmann had a high pitched speaking voice and delivered messages without emotion. Aging, balding, and be-speckled, he was friendly and approachable away from the pulpit but a little difficult for me to follow during the sermons. I began praying and looking for an encounter with the Living God during these sermons. Sometimes, a particular message spoke to me and sometimes it was difficult to keep from falling asleep. Suppose I snored or drooled! That would have been mortifying.

The children's Sunday school was conducted at the same time as the adult church and so they did not attend the preaching along with their parents and other adults. Mrs. Hornsby continued to teach Sunday school and so I did not see her until after church.

One day I invited Mrs. Hornsby and her husband to dinner. Colonel Thurman Hornsby was a career military officer who met his wife in France fifteen years earlier. Frequently absent from her side, he was off serving in other parts of the world. They were magnificent to observe when they were together. After ten years of marriage he remained close to her side, glancing at her often and she would return his glance with a smile. They shared a subtle intimacy that spoke of the sweetest kind of love.

The Colonel didn't seem as comfortable around children as did his wife. His military bearing was slightly more rigid and his facial expression tense when the children were close. Mrs. Hornsby was very relaxed with them. She touched their faces and stroked their hair when she read to them. Children were drawn to her.

After getting to know the couple more, she told me the story of how they met. He was a young officer stationed in France and she was an art student during the War. The first time they met was a formal dinner given by her father before the occupation, but had no subsequent contact until VE Day. Parties throughout Paris on VE Day meant hundreds of thousands of people crowded into the streets, taverns, and halls to celebrate. They were introduced again at a celebration at the university but were separated after a few dances by the throngs of people pressing in around them. The, then, Captain searched for her for days having only her name and description. He admitted he had forgotten who her father was and where he lived. Days later he found her studying in the library and began a year-long courtship. Collette Genevieve was the daughter of a wealthy businessman who did not approve of the marriage. The couple eloped and eventually he brought his bride to America.

The couple had remained childless and she had resigned herself to those circumstances and spent as much time as she could around other people's children. The Colonel would not consider adopting a child.

Although we became friends, I continued to call her Mrs.

Hornsby because she called me Dr. Aldridge, and just would not use my given name. Her accent was barely noticeable.

From that time on, when the Colonel was back home in Cincinnati the couple would invite me to go with them out to dinner or an orchestra concert or a play or some other event that required formal dress.

She and I would go to art museums, botanical gardens, or book store openings together when the Colonel was away. Sometimes she would call me and ask me to go shopping with her. The stores that we shopped were more elite than I could afford but I enjoyed window shopping.

Wives of the other doctors with whom I worked were friendly enough, but there was a slight sense that they may have felt threatened just as Mrs. Nastasic had been. If they were, they were not so obvious about it. Mostly they just didn't know how to relate to me. So, at gatherings, I associated with the other doctors to discuss events of the day such as politics, medical concerns and research, and the Communist threat. For the most part these were less than enjoyable gatherings for me. I was out of place no matter with which group I associated.

CHAPTER 21

Vernon Blotch

In the mid-spring of 1958, a young man was rushed into the emergency room after falling from a tractor and getting caught in the cultivating machine. His left leg was badly mangled and upon further assessment we found that the bone had been shattered. His brother had put a tourniquet on the leg preventing him from bleeding to death as the artery had been severely lacerated.

I had to emergently repair the arterial laceration but the femur was splintered and could not be fixed enough to mend the bone. He was taken to surgery and the orthopedic surgeon amputated his leg.

Through his hospitalization, I followed him after the orthopedic surgeon signed off of the case. The young man's name was Vernon Blotch. Vernon was from Harrison. His family had a medium sized farm that Vernon worked whenever he wasn't in school. Vernon was a large fifteen year old farm-boy. He was interested in girls, cars, and football, but not necessarily in that order. He didn't like school but didn't mind working on the farm, if it could earn him a little spending money to take a girl to a movie.

"I just want to buy a good car, is all I want," he once told me.

His biggest ambition at age fifteen was to drive. A few weeks later, he was devastated when his brother told him that he couldn't drive with only one leg. Driving took two feet to manage clutch, brake, and gas pedals, or so he thought.

After this, Vernon withdrew from everyone. He stopped going to physical therapy and clamped his mouth shut to avoid crying. I brought him magazines that featured newer model cars that advertised automatic transmissions. He showed little interest in the new cars.

"New cars cost a lot of money. I will never be able to work to save money to buy one of those." He grew angry, and refused to be comforted, even by his mother. He threw trays of food when they were presented to him.

This went on for several weeks. Other doctors advised me to discharge him since he refused to do what he needed to do to get better. Elaine came in to see him at my request. Initially he was too angry to work with her. She checked in with him, faithfully, every day. She would not be the one to give up on him.

"Vernon," I sat down in a chair next to his bed, "What do you want to happen?" I asked him.

"I want my leg back," he spat out.

"OK, that's not going to happen. What do you want to happen next?" I asked.

"I want everyone to leave me alone," he growled.

"OK, that's not going to happen, either. So what do you want to happen?" I persisted.

He was quiet for a moment. "I don't know." He admitted. Adolescents often don't know what they want from life, or they do know at one moment and are unsure the next under the best of circumstances. Life altering changes are very confusing for them.

"You want to drive, this much I know. You will be able to drive. You will. You will walk, too, if you do the work now." I aimed to frame these ideas around what could happen when he tried and not what could happen if he gave up. "Look at the man in this picture, Vernon." I showed him a picture in a frame. "You see this man? He is missing his left leg just like you."

At first Vernon didn't want to look at the picture, afraid of what he might see. But he was curious and after a minute, stretched his neck to look at the photo.

"Yeah?" he said.

"Yes. He lost it during the first War when a soldier next to him stepped on a landmine. That man was killed and this fellow lost his leg. How does he look to you in this picture?"

"Did he get his leg blown off after this picture was taken?"

"Nope. He is missing his leg in that picture." I said. "You can't see that though. He has a pretty good prosthetic leg. He calls it his 'wooden leg' but it's not made out of wood. Do you know what else? He drives cars with clutches. He learned how many years ago. Sometimes he has a little trouble if he has to stop on a hill but you know what, a lot of people do, don't they?"

"I guess so," he answered. "Who is the baby he's holding?"

"That's me. Wasn't I cute?" I joked. "He's my father. After the War, he met my mother. They had four children. Not having a leg hasn't stopped him from doing just about anything he wanted to do."

Normally, I never talked to patients or their families about my private life. It isn't professional but sometimes the need outweighed the principle. A child this age wants to exercise his independence and doesn't want to be thought of as just another child. They, at once want to be thought of as different, their own person, and not different from other children. Conformist and non-conformist! A missing limb marked him as different but not in the way he would want to be known.

"Do you know any other farm boys who are missing arms, or legs? It is a common farm accident." I offered. If he knew of another child or adult there could be misconceptions, mocking or embarrassment over it. Elaine or I could help him reframe his thinking.

"Yeah. Jeff Conley fell into a thrasher and his right arm is gone up to the elbow. There's Robbie Smith. He got an infection in his foot when he stepped on a spike and they cut it off. Then there's Elmer Rauch got his eye knocked out with pellet gun. I probably know a half dozen other guys who had something happen. Robbie can drive cuz he can use his leg to push the clutch in. But my whole leg is gone, all the way up. I'm disgusting." He disparaged.

"You are not disgusting, Vernon. You are the same person you always were. Are you the kind of person to give up just because things are difficult?"

"This is not just difficult," he argued.

"How well do you know Jeff and Robbie and the other fellows? I'm sure they got discouraged when these things first happened. There's a lot of pain and some failures before you overcome the circumstances. But if you want to you can do it. Talk to these guys. Ask them." I would have loved to have my father come and talk to this young man, but that would be over-the-line for certain. My Papa would not think so though.

"Will you do it, Vernon?" I pleaded.

"Maybe."

This was an encouraging sign. He didn't completely reject the idea. I don't know if he ever did as I asked but he began eating, going to physical therapy and was casted for the prosthetic once the swelling went down, which is the first step in the process. Vernon met with Elaine and shared his concerns and hopes with her.

Because Vernon was from Harrison, I was reminded about the airport out there. The next week end that I had free I made a trip over to talk to someone and sign up for lessons. The airport was pretty far off the beaten path and I took some wrong turns at several places along the way but the memories of being in Jasper Jenkins's airplane kept pushing me to go on until I found the place.

Harrison Airport had two Quonset hut hangers, and an office and one grass runway. A small monoplane was taking off as I drove up. In the heavily rutted gravel parking area there were six cars and a pickup truck parked all askew.

One nice looking, leathery-skinned fellow with dark hair, greying slightly at the edges, directed me to ask for Henry in the office. The wall of the sparsely furnished office sported a variety of pin-up calendars, and out in front of a long counter, two long tables, six steel chairs and a wooden swivel chair in which sat the rotund Henry. He was talking to a busty red haired woman in a tight pink sweater. He smiled when I walked in and asked if he could help me.

"I have spoken to you over the telephone, I believe. You told me that there are flight instructors here and that I could take lessons."

Henry leaned forward in his swivel chair and laughed a hardy belly laugh. "I told *you* that *you* could take lessons?"

"Well, yes. You said there are instructors that would use their own airplanes to give lessons."

"Yeah. There are certified flight instructors, but honey you ain't got the right equipment," his tone was crude.

"That may be, but the color of my money should be the right color. There *are* female pilots," my tone defiant. I probably wasn't making a friend in Henry.

He laughed even harder. The woman he was with pursed her lips in disapproval. I wasn't sure if she disapproved of my pursuit of flying or Henry's denigration of our sex. I didn't care.

"What's your name, sweetheart?"

"Doctor Rebecca Aldridge." boasting about my title, but I felt I had earned a little respect.

"Well, *Doctor* Rebecca Aldridge, I'll just introduce you to Bill Boyette. He was a fly boy in the service. *MAYBE* he would like the color of your money, but don't count on it," Henry laughed as he spoke.

Mr. Boyette was the dark handsome man that had pointed me in the direction of the office. Initially he was pleasant when Henry introduced us, but his tone changed when he heard why I had come.

"Are you kidding me?" he barked. "What makes you think you can handle one of these? I earned my wings the hard way flying missions over Germany. A woman shouldn't be at the controls when it gets rough up there."

"I'll tell you what makes me think I can handle it. One of the best pilots I ever knew told me that he thought I could do it. He would let me take the control in his Stearman and *he* wasn't scared that I would crash him. Is *that* your problem?"

Enraged he shouted "Scared!? Me!? You must be crazy, lady coming here and calling me scared."

"Then why won't you take the challenge of teaching me? Jasper earned his wings the hard way, too. If he hadn't gotten sick I would have asked him to teach me."

Listening to our conversation, a man who had been standing nearby, interrupted us. "Jasper who?" he directed the question to me.

"Jasper Jenkins. I grew up riding in his airplane," these statements were certainly exaggerated. He never told me directly that he thought that I had what it takes to pilot an airplane. He never let me take the controls, but he did tell someone that he thought I could do it.

All three men got quiet for a moment. Tony was the man who had asked the question.

"I'll teach you. I'll do it for nothing." Tony said. The general attitude toward me seemed to have changed. The name of Jasper Jenkins struck a chord in these men. "Maybe she can teach *us* something, Bill."

"Is that old war horse still around? That codger must be a hunerd years old by now," was Henry's comment.

"No he passed away a couple of years ago."

"Tony," Henry continued "if you have a heart attack up there or something this here little lady's a doctor."

Tony was in his mid-thirties and in pretty good shape. He was not likely to have a heart attack. Bill was older, maybe in his late fifties and also in pretty good shape. Henry was probably in his sixties, at my estimation and at least seventy-five pounds overweight. He huffed and puffed as he walked and his face was as red as a beet. He was the most likely candidate for a heart attack.

"Oh, a doctor, huh? Maybe I *will* charge you for lessons, after all," Tony said with a big grin.

"I don't care who she knew," Bill grouched "women shouldn't be up there flying," He walked away toward the hanger.

Tony Mansfield had been flying since his early twenties and became a certified flight instructor (CFI) just four years later, after he had put in over 9,000 hours in the air. His occupation was crop duster. Tony owned two airplanes; a crop duster and a 1949 Cessna 170A which was a high winged all metal aircraft. The later was the type that he used to teach new pilots.

Throughout the morning there were flurries of activity with pilots taking off and landing, fueling up and tying down airplanes.

That same day, Tony took me up in his Cessna. A closed cockpit was a very different experience than flying in Mr. Jenkins open cockpit biplane so many years earlier, but it was not disappointing.

My heart raced as he pulled back on the throttle to take us down the runway to reach the necessary speed to lift off of the ground. Gravity pushed us deeper into our seats and he pulled back on the stick to gain altitude. The nose of the plane rose and we climbed above the tree tops, and continued to climb. Everything below diminished as the vastness of the sky increased. Tony leveled the plane off and gravity seemed to fade away.

He banked to the left and I gazed to my left past Tony looking down at the world below. Woods and clearings, fields and houses, when viewed from above seemed small; when in fact they were large woods, clearings and fields.

"Have you seen Cincinnati from the air?" he asked.

"No," I yelled above the engine noise.

"You will now," he declared.

Tony continued to bank her around until he flew back over the airfield from which we had just taken off. He leveled off again. Within minutes I could see the wide brown ribbon; the Ohio River. He followed the river until the city came into view. The buildings and various structures crowded closer and closer together as we approached the big city.

The Roebling suspension bridge gleamed blue in the sunshine. Steel buildings and silver windows flashed the sun's rays at us here and there.

"You need to come see this at night. Spectacular when it's all lit up," he broke the silence. "There's Crosley field."

He dropped altitude for a better look. A few minutes later he said "I think…yeah…that's the university."

"So many church spires," I commented, then "Oh!" as I spotted the half domed arch of the Union Terminal. "The train station," I said. It was even more magnificent from the air. A few times around the city and then it was time to return to Harrison.

The return to the small airport was quiet with only the

drone of the engine in the background to remind me how it was that I could be in the sky. It was all so wonderful and made me anxious to learn to do it myself. Joystick forward, I could dive; joystick back, I could climb; bank left and the left wing dipped; bank right and the right wing dipped as if extensions of myself. Given the controls I would become the bird I was flying.

Ground school commenced the following week and I completed that straight away. The plan was to begin in-flight lessons immediately but life and my work got in the way. It took me months to get through the requirements but eventually I did solo.

Tony watched my take-offs and landings from the windsock early in the mornings when the air was most calm, confident in his teaching ability. I could hear his instructions in my head as though he was beside me.

A few short cross country solo flights allowed me to calculate fuel needs, plot courses, navigate and experience other airports and runways.

The written pilot's exam was not difficult compared to taking medical boards and I was equally at ease for the in-flight practical exam with the examiner. I passed and received my private pilot's license. The next step would be to save enough money for my own airplane.

The very next Saturday, after receiving my license I took Willa and her brother and sister to the airport. I had been flying solo now for months and had been promising to take them up in the airplane. The children's excitement reignited my own. Not that I would ever tire of flying, everything about it thrilled me. It was the honor of sharing the real-life experience with someone who before had only dreamed about it.

The first to go up with me was Willa. It was to be her fledgling eagle view of God's creation.

Five planes were lined up wing-tip to wing-tip outside

of the hanger. Willa and her siblings ran toward the row of planes.

"Which one is it, Dr. Becka?" Willa could not contain her excitement.

"The blue and white one," I shouted as they had gotten a distance ahead of me.

Tony wandered out of the office to greet us. We had made the arrangements to use his airplane weeks before.

"Are you guys excited about going up?" he asked the children.

"Yeah!" they all shouted in unison.

"Are you scared?" he asked.

"A little," said Willa.

"Naw. Not me," said Jerry.

"I am," said Joanie.

"Well, you needn't worry. This here is my airplane. I take good care of it to keep it safe. I fly it nearly every day so you better believe I'm gunna make sure everything works properly. And I trust Becka, here, with it. I taught her to fly myself," he smiled and winked at Joanie.

She smiled nervously back. The pep talk didn't help her very much. Her expression grew grimmer. "Joanie, you'll go up last OK? Then once Willa and Jerry go up they will tell you what it's like. They are going to be just as excited when they come back down as they are right now," I told her.

"OK," her face relaxed, relieved to go last.

Willa and Jerry checked out Tony's plane up close. Neither one had ever been near an airplane before, but both had gone to the library to find everything they could on the subject.

"It looks small," Jerry commented "What's the wing span?"

"About twenty five feet," Tony answered.

"The Spirit of Saint Louis was forty six feet. Can this cross the ocean?" he asked.

"Nope," Tony answered.

Bill Boyette had been close by tinkering with his engine and overheard the conversation. He snorted loudly enough that the child could hear him and shook his head. It was enough to make Jerry stop asking questions.

I told Jerry all about the Cessna that we would be flying, when it was built and what it could do. Jerry just wanted to be a part of everything. He had not intended to sound like a know-it-all. Bill seemed to not like children any more than he liked women pilots .This is not to say that he didn't like women. He had many female admirers who came to watch him fly and compete in air race competitions.

The children followed me into the office as I logged in and checked on the flying conditions. Jerry's eyes grew wide when he noticed the half-nude pin-up calendars on the wall but he didn't say anything about them. Jerry and Joanie remained in the office with some snacks from the vending machine as Willa and I went out for her first flight.

The Cessna had been rolled out to the runway and was waiting for us. Tony helped Willa into the passenger side and buckled her into her seat. He smiled and patted her head. She hadn't stopped smiling since we got into the car at her mother's house.

Although Tony did a walk-around inspection of the plane, I did my own just as he had taught me. Then I climbed into the pilot's seat which elicited a thrill for me that never got old.

Willa was less interested in the airplane and the procedures than Jerry and more interested in leaving the earth underfoot and soaring through the sky. Willa wanted to become a pilot just like me. I didn't tell her, at that time, about some of the restrictions. A pilot had to have perfect vision in both eyes. Willa would not qualify for a pilot's license. So, I kept quiet and I just let her enjoy the experience of flying.

"You told Sister Elaine once that if you could be any

animal you wanted you would be an eagle, remember? Is this close enough?" I asked her.

"You remembered that?" she seemed amazed that I remembered.

"Of course, because that was my answer, too."

Jerry and Willa enjoyed the flight immensely but Joanie was frightened and did not enjoy it. I decided that in the future that she could remain on the ground and have snacks and play on the pool table that was back in the airport office.

CHAPTER 22
Hank Leaves His Family

On May 29, 1958 Heidi called me at ten o'clock in the evening. She was crying hysterically.

"Hank has left us, Becka. He told me he wants a divorce," she was crying too hard for me to understand what she said next. The telephone connection was more staticy than usual making it that much more difficult to understand her.

"Are you alone now?"

"He left us. He took his…" more incomprehensible talk.

"Is your mother with you, Sweetheart?" My heart was breaking that she was too far away for me to put my arms around her, even though I knew that it wasn't me she needed.

"No," she sobbed.

"I'm so, so sorry, Heidi," I was crying too.

"I did everything he ever wanted. I tried so hard…"

Mitch and the baby were crying in the background. Lily's cries were shrill and piercing. The house must have been in such turmoil for the little ones to be so disquieted at that hour. Their cries were coming from a little distance from her. I could tell that she was not holding either one of them.

"Where are the children right now?" I asked.

"I shut them in their rooms. I can't get them to stop crying. They were so scared. Hank and I were screaming at each other. I'm such a bad mother. My poor babies!"

"Talk to me a minute and then go take a look at them. OK? Make sure they didn't get themselves into any trouble. Now, are you safe? He didn't hurt you or the children, did he?" I asked prepared to hang up and call Mr. Anderson.

"No. He didn't hurt us. He never, ever raised a hand to me," she was beginning to sound a little more in control.

I thought, no, he just abused you psychologically.

"Good. Good. Take a deep breath," I instructed. This was not intended to be virtual, but literal. I heard her breath in and hold it for a long time. "Breathe, Shug," I encouraged. She exhaled.

"We need to get you someone there, right now. You shouldn't be alone. Oh, sugar I wish I was there."

"I do, too," her voice trembled but she was understandable.

"I want you to hang up and go check on the babies. I am going to call your mother. Is that OK?" I asked permission because I didn't understand why she hadn't called her before she called me.

"OK," then she hung up first.

Mrs. Anderson's breathless, shaky voice made her sound frightened when she answered the telephone. Late night calls in our little town usually weren't a good omen. She didn't sound surprised to hear the news; only that it came from me instead of from Heidi. I couldn't tell her why Heidi had called me first instead of her. Heidi might have feared judgment from her mother. Since the baby had been born Mrs. Anderson had been there any time that Heidi needed her. She was doting on her grandchildren, but I didn't know family business and so didn't know the dynamic between Heidi and her mother.

Most of what I learned about what became of a once close

relationship between Heidi and her mother, George told me. He loved them both and he wished he could fix the distance that developed between them.

She agreed to go to her daughter immediately and she made Mr. Anderson go with her.

Heidi sounded a little calmer when I called back. Mitch was quiet and the baby was cooing close to the telephone and I assumed that she was being held by her mother.

"Your mother and father are on their way. I think I hear Lily. How are the children?" I inquired.

"Mitch is sleeping beside me here on the couch. Yes, Lily is right here looking at me and smiling. Such a sweet smile," mama cooed back at her baby.

"So, tell me what happened."

"Hank just came home late; after the kids were in bed, and he had been drinking. He's been acting odd lately but I try not to nag him. I know that his job is demanding," she told me. I wondered how often he had used that as an excuse, as those were the same words he gave me about his behavior.

"Out of the blue he told me that he wants a divorce and that he had already spoken to a friend of his that is a divorce lawyer."

"Did he say why he wanted a divorce?"

"He said he couldn't do this anymore. It's all too much with the baby the way she is and the responsibility of the family and the job. He said he doesn't love me anymore," she choked back the words.

No words of comfort for her came to me. There was no excuse for a grown man to abandon this responsibility.

"Do you think if Papa talked to him he could help him sort it all out?" It wasn't much but it was the first thing that came to my mind. Hank went to church. He seemed to have respect for Papa.

"If he doesn't love me anymore, what can your Papa do to change that?" she begged.

"Maybe he doesn't mean it. I'm not going to make excuses for him, Heidi. Someone needs to talk to him and your father probably isn't the best choice for that. I'm sure he will have a lot to say to Hank. But I'm not sure it will help the situation."

"There's no love lost between Daddy and Hank," she snorted. Was she suppressing a laugh?

We talked for thirty minutes until her parents arrived. She had gotten control of herself and spoke calmly while still sniffing at times.

The urge to take off and drive to her was so strong, nearly irresistible, but I still had obligations that could not be ignored. But after Hank left, Heidi and I spoke on the telephone every day and sometimes more often than once a day. I spoke to Mrs. Anderson daily as well and was glad to hear her defending her daughter in every way.

I made plans to drive back home as soon as I could make arrangements. It would be two weeks. Dr. Nastasic would cover the office and the hospital approved the time off for me.

It had been nearly a two years since I had been home. Lorelei and Sully were getting pretty serious if Papa gaged everything correctly. Everyone else was doing well, except for Heidi.

Tony allowed me to use his Cessna and since school was finished for the year I asked Mrs. Lockhart if Willa could come with me. She agreed and Willa was ecstatic about the idea.

Vernon would be close to discharge by that time. He balanced well with his temporary prosthetic and was taking steps clumsily. Within two weeks, if he continued to work he would be ready to go home. Harrison, where he lived, was close to the airport; so on those days whenever I went flying I planned to stop in to check on his progress.

CHAPTER 23

Back Home in Belmont

There were no big surprise parties when I returned home this time. I had begged Papa after the last time that they would not do that again and he agreed. One of the best parts of the last visit was dearly missed during this one. George couldn't come home to visit.

Matt and his family drove down to spend time with us. Ginny was five months pregnant with child number four. Both parents took it in stride but Ginny had admitted to me years earlier that she wanted a large family. "As many as the good Lord gives us. We will love them all."

MJ, Danny, and Emily were growing as expected. An aunt shouldn't have favorites, and indeed, I loved them all, but Paul was special to me. Even though he had never known his father, he grew into the young man that his father had been. He was quiet, considerate of others, slightly impulsive at times but not angry like Aaron. His mother's gentle influence had shown strong in him.

Matt had volunteered to pick us up at the small airport just a few miles outside of Belmont. He had another new gigantic

Cadillac which was becoming his pattern. He got a new car about every other year. His home in Raleigh was also ostentatious but Ginny made it a comfortable and hospitable place to visit but it had been several years since I had been there.

Everyone else was waiting for us at Papa's house. Anxious to get to Heidi, I excused myself after I said hello to everyone and took our suitcases up to my room. Lorelei begged to come with me. She had been out to help Heidi as often as she could and had grown close to her. Willa stayed with Papa, Paul, and Matt and his family.

We drove Papa's car and left together promising not to be long but I couldn't keep that promise.

Mrs. Cordray, a friend of Mrs. Anderson, answered Heidi's door when we arrived.

"How is she?" I asked her.

"She's resting, Rebecca. Still not doing too good, poor dear!"

"Is she awake? Can I go in and see her?"

"You know you can. She has been looking forward to you coming home. Go on in," Mrs. Cordray instructed me and pointed the way to the bedroom. Lorelei didn't follow me, but instead went into the room where Mitch was playing.

Lying motionless on the bed, Heidi opened her eyes when I came into the room. Her hair was a nest of wisps and mats barely contained by a couple of barrettes. Wearing no make-up, and sunken cheeks and puffy eyes made her look old. During our conversations over the telephone she never sounded as bad as she looked right then.

I sat beside her on the bed and rubbed her back. I could tell that she was dehydrated by her dry, wrinkled skin. She had no tears when she cried.

What words could have been spoken to take away her pain? I felt like Job's friends who sat with him in the ashes after he had lost everything. In the Bible Job lost his family, his riches and his health. His friends just sat with him for a while not saying anything. But once they opened their mouths they made things so much worse.

I prayed silently *Where are you, Lord? My friend is in pain. She is a good, faithful person. Why is this happening to her? Please, Lord, please bring her comfort. If you love her as much as I do, please don't let her suffer like this.*

A thought that was not my own spoke to me over and over. "Daughter, I *do* love her. *Be* her friend," it said.

I held her and wept.

Finally, she spoke to me. "I'm so glad you're here," and she reached around my neck and held onto me.

It struck me how thin she had become. While I was far away I could imagine that she was going to be alright through all of this. No one had prepared me for what I saw. I was a healer and this helpless feeling was intolerable.

There was nothing I could *do*. I could only *be*. Intolerable or not I was where she needed me to be.

"Do you think the alcohol is why my baby is like she is?" she asked hesitantly. I immediately regretted ever having said anything back then.

"Do you think you are being punished for something? You told me yourself that you knew women who drank and their babies were alright. I've seen babies with cerebral palsy and their mother's didn't drink a drop. Don't do that to yourself. You didn't hurt your baby. I'm pretty sure my mother never touched a drink in her life, and Benji was born like he was. No! No! I don't think any such thing."

She settled back down and withdrew into herself.

The light through the window was beginning to fade into hues of yellow and pink. Soon it was dark. It was difficult to tell the time when Mrs. Cordray came in with a tray on which she had placed Heidi's best tea set with Chamomile tea and some broth.

"Heidi, do you want to eat something now?" she pleaded.

"I'm not hungry Mrs. Cordray. Thank you just the same," she said as she lay back down with her head on the pillow and turned away from the door.

"You must eat something. Mitch is getting so big. If you don't eat you won't be able to pick that child up. He still likes hugs, doesn't he?" I asked.

"I would imagine," she responded distantly.

I insisted she sit up and I spooned some of the broth into her mouth. As long as she accepted it, I kept feeding it to her. She only accepted about a quarter of a cup before stopping. "Has Dr. Stanton been over to see you?" I asked.

"I don't think so," she answered.

"I want him to see you. Have you eaten or drank anything lately?"

"I don't remember."

It had been only about two weeks since Hank left. If she stopped taking fluids at that time she could be in trouble. "I'll be back in a minute," I told her and went to find Mrs. Cordray and Lorelei.

"Has she been like this since Hank left?" I asked them both.

"Not this bad until a few days ago when the divorce papers came," Mrs. Cordray explained.

"She's clinically depressed. We need Dr. Stanton to come and see her tonight," I told them.

He was called and came within fifteen minutes. He agreed with my assessment that she was extremely dehydrated and needed intravenous fluids right away. If she refused to go to the hospital we could start an IV there, but if I could get her to agree to go to the hospital we would have access to quick laboratory results that could give us better information as to how bad she was, and if it had affected her kidneys.

Heidi didn't disagree so we made arrangements to get her

to the hospital right away. Mrs. Anderson came to the house to watch the children.

Once in the hospital, Heidi improved mentally after she had been given three liters of IV fluids. She remained depressed but no damage had been done to her kidneys. I stayed with her overnight.

Mrs. Anderson had coordinated around the clock care of Heidi and the grandchildren since Hank left providing most of the care herself. She, too, looked haggard and exhausted from worry. A remarkably strong woman, she never complained about the pain she experienced from her severe arthritis or the emotional pain she felt for her daughter. Anger expressed itself on her usually kind face whenever the mention of Hank's name came up, but she refrained from commenting. It was not her nature to speak directly unkind words but she had a way to backhandedly let you know how she felt. Like when she told George that he and I had made our own choices that took us separate ways and that it was a "good choice."

I loved her, even if she didn't love me anymore. Of this, I couldn't be certain, though.

Papa attempted to speak to Hank but Hank wouldn't return his calls nor answer the door at the walk-up apartment he had rented in town. Word had come back to Mr. Anderson through his network of "spies" that Hank was preparing to leave his brother's law practice and move out of the area. To a small town, this was a scandal.

He was not sending money to Heidi for her or the children to pay bills nor buy food. The church family stood in the gap to help her with everything that she needed. Papa said "The Lord is providing for their needs."

Could it be that simple? They needed more. But for the time being, child care, housekeeping, cooking and a lot of love were sustaining them. Papa told me, "God can be trusted."

Lily's limitations were beginning to become obvious. Her

development was delayed. She didn't reach or grasp things like a nearly two year old. She didn't scoot across the floor nor babble. But she engaged by looking intently at whoever spoke to her and her precious facial expressions lead one to believe she was deeply considering anything that was said to her. In my mind, I could never imagine what was going through Hank's mind, as he rejected this lovely little girl.

Mitch was now six years old and had started school and was doing well. I was amazed at his maturity. His deep blue eyes were wise beyond his years. He could read and often read to Lily. Hank had likely influenced his vocabulary, which was extensive. All in all, he was an extremely bright boy. And he still adored his baby sister.

After playing for fifteen to twenty minutes he would come to wherever little Lily was to check and see if she was alright. He spoke to her in his little adult fashion, never baby talk like some of the adults. He would sometimes correct adults if they deliberately mispronounced a word or talked baby talk to her. He didn't ask about his father, nor speak as if he expected him to come back to him. Mitch talked about his father, about what kind of work he did, or what he said about a subject.

The day before his mother was to be discharged to come home, he climbed up on the couch beside me as I held Lily. He leaned over my lap and turned his head up to look at my face.

"Are you a doctor?" he asked.

"Yes. I am, Mitch. I am a doctor for babies and children."

He had an astonished look on his face. "Is something wrong with Lily?" he asked, innocently.

"I think she is a sweet little baby girl. Why? Did someone tell you there is something wrong with her?"

"Daddy says she ain't right."

"Well, I think she is right for who she is. Do you think there is something wrong with her?" I wondered if Hank had tainted his view of her.

"Naw. I don't know why he said that. She looks just fine."

"I have seen people who look just fine and aren't right. I have seen a lot of people who look different who are nice and kind and sweet. Sometimes the people who look right have meanness inside them that makes them not right. Lily is nice and sweet and I think she will be just like you. She loves her big brother."

I told him the story of my three brothers and how important they were to me. I told him that his Uncle George is his mommy's big brother and how he always was good to her and helped her.

Mitch was satisfied with my answers and rubbed Lily's tummy and sang her a song before running off to play again.

When Heidi came home she remained a little weak but she rushed through the door to hug her babies. "I have missed you so much," she told Mitch as she lifted him off of the floor.

"Mama, don't hug me so tight," he pleaded. She relaxed her arms a little bit without letting him go.

After a minute she turned to me and put her arms out for Lily. "You didn't forget me did you, sweet girl?" she said to her toddler. Lily smiled up at her not forgotten mother, and Heidi collapsed onto the couch with her baby in her arms. She had only been gone days, but she had been emotionally absent from them for several weeks.

I spent a part of every day that I had left in Belmont at Heidi's home. Mrs. Anderson continued to coordinate women who would come and help her out without overwhelming her with numbers of people at once.

Papa's home was a refuge for me, no matter what else was going on. The next week after I came home while Matt and his family were still there, Lorelei and Sully made an announcement at the dinner table. Papa had been expecting them to finally tell everyone how they felt about each other.

Sully stood up and took a deep breath before speaking.

"Reverend Aldridge, I would like to marry Lorelei. I know she is like your daughter and so I want to ask your blessing," he breathed out, relieved to have gotten the words out.

Lorelei smiled and looked down shyly.

"Well, what did *she* say about it, Sully?" Papa teased.

"Wah…she…said yes," he stammered. It was sweet that he seemed at a loss for words. That was uncharacteristic for him.

"What did Paul say?" Papa asked next. Everyone looked at Paul who straightened up and grinned. Willa seemed enthralled with Paul. Her face just lit up whenever he looked at her. She sat quietly beside Paul.

Paul didn't answer the question because the question was directed to Sully.

"Uhm…Uhm…Guess I didn't ask him," Sully looked at Paul for a moment "Well, can I marry your mother?" he asked most sincerely.

Paul answered "It's about time," and laughed.

"When is this going to happen?" I nudged Lorelei.

"We were thinking about Christmas time. Do you think you can come back around then?" she asked me.

"I don't know how much time I can get but I will be here for a wedding." I answered.

She seemed embarrassed at the thought of a wedding. "I wasn't thinking of a wedding; more like a little ceremony. But I want you with me, you know, to stand up with me in case I faint or something," she giggled.

"I'll be there," I reassured her.

Everyone congratulated Sully, getting out of their seats and shaking his hand or slapping him on the back.

Paul and Willa had become quick friends. Paul was seventeen and Willa had just turned fifteen. He asked me a lot of questions about Willa whenever we were alone. My answers were always "You need to ask her yourself."

She wasn't secretive about what had happened to her, but

it wasn't something she shared with everyone. The scars on her face were barely noticeable but her prosthetic eye was detectable and there was a slight unevenness to the bone around her left eye. She was still pretty and more confident than I had ever been. The one interest that Paul and Willa had in common was music. Paul played just about any instrument that he could get his hands on and Willa sang like an angel. Paul decided to write some songs for her and send them to her back in Cincinnati.

When I had to return to Cincinnati, things weren't ideal, but Heidi was being cared for and Papa and my family were happy.

CHAPTER 24
Sally Sullivan

Fifteen-year-old, Sally Sullivan had to be helped into the treatment room of our office by her father. She looked like a living skeleton. Nurse Hanson had to assist her onto the scale to get her height and weight. She raised the height bar to the top of Sally's head. She was five foot four inches tall. She then slid the weight slide across the bottom horizontal bar but had to slide it back to zero. The bottom bar started at one hundred pounds. She slid the top slide and tapped it back to record a reading of sixty-five pounds. Sally's pulse bounded when I put my two fingers on her wrist. Then, when I listened to her heart with my stethoscope it beat wildly and I heard a swishing sound which meant she had a murmur. Her hair and nails were dry and brittle and patches of hair were missing from her scalp. I heard gurgling noises when listening over her abdomen which was normal and expected. She winced, when I pushed on the right side of her belly and felt an enlarged liver.

Sally denied belly pain, bloody or clay color stools, or bloody or dark colored urine. When I asked her if she had any change in appetite, she said no, but her father said angrily, "She won't eat anything. She is starving herself to death."

"How long has it been since she refused to eat?" I inquired.

He hesitated for a moment then said "I don't really know. She's been living with her mother. I haven't seen her for months. I found her yesterday and grabbed her away from my ex-wife."

"Sally, why don't you want to eat?" I asked.

"I don't want to get fat," she confessed.

I took her father out of the exam room and told him that I needed to put her into the hospital immediately. Her anorexia had already affected her liver, and very likely other organs.

"She is a very sick girl," I told him.

"I know. Please help her," he begged.

Sally was transported to the hospital by ambulance from my office and admitted directly to the medical floor. The tests and X-rays showed organ failure of her kidneys and liver, demineralization of the bones and an enlarged heart. Her heart had been working hard to compensate for the failure of the other organs.

The diagnosis of Anorexia Nervosa was a psychiatric diagnosis but her medical condition was critical at this point and the psychiatric issue would have to be addressed if she could be stabilized. An intravenous line was placed to hydrate her and a tube was placed down her nose to her stomach to begin providing nutrition. The tube feeding was tricky since her stomach would reject too much too soon. In the meantime, we initiated replacement of calories, electrolytes and minerals that could be given via IV or intramuscular injections.

Sally vomited every time we put even the smallest amount of liquefied food down the tube. She also started having constant diarrhea which meant that we had to replace even more fluid by IV. Her skin was eroding away around her rectum because of the diarrhea and caused her a lot of pain.

After two days she was nearly too weak to speak. She seemed to concentrate on just breathing. Sally would answer questions if she was asked, but we tried to keep those to a minimum. At one point she reached for my hand and asked "Can I see my mother?"

I told her I would see what I could do.

Taking her father aside, I told him "Sally remains unstable. When the body chemistry is this out of balance sometimes it is difficult to correct it. We will continue to treat her aggressively, but you should know that there is a possibility she may not turn around. She has asked for her mother. Do you know where she is? She should be allowed to come and see her."

Mr. Sullivan became very angry with me at this suggestion. He was an imposing figure, tall and wide. He looked very strong, but in spite of that he was helpless to do anything for his daughter.

"Her mother is the one who let it get this out of hand. I'm not going to let her come and see Sally. She let this happen. She didn't get help when it started," he bellowed.

"Her mother can't make decisions for her at this point, that's up to you, but Sally has asked for her. Don't punish Sally because you are angry at her mother."

"I'll talk to Sally," he pushed passed me to go into her room.

Later, I approached him again. "Mr. Sullivan, Sally has a psychiatric condition that caused this problem. She sees herself through a distorted mental lens. We can see that she is far too skinny but she sees herself as fat. When she is stable she will need to see the psychiatrist. It is an illness not a character flaw. An illness," I emphasized. "You wouldn't judge a child because they have diabetes or cancer. Her mother didn't do it to her. Mental illness is not something that someone else can give to a person. Did you talk to Sally about her mother?"

"Yeah. She wants to see her. I don't want her to see Sally," he grew more agitated as he spoke. "All she had to do was to take her to a doctor. Anyone could see that she was starving herself," Mr. Sullivan punched the wall and knocked a hole in it. Ken, one of the orderlies came running over.

"Are you alright, Dr. Aldridge?" he raised his voice. "Is this man threating you?"

"No, Ken. It's alright. Mr. Sullivan is upset, but he's calmed down now," I more instructed Mr. Sullivan, than answered Ken. Then I took Mr. Sullivan's hand to see if he had injured himself. His knuckles were red but no cuts and nothing to indicate broken bones.

"You need to calm down. We will do everything we can for Sally. You need to do everything you can for Sally as well. All I ask is that you *think* about what we said. You make the decision about what is best there. Alright?" I spoke very calmly.

"Yeah. OK," he answered and turned and walked away. After he went home, I went in Sally's room to check on her.

Her appearance was always so startling. Her muscles were so wasted away that her jaw, cheek bones and brow looked like sharp blades. As she breathed her shoulders heaved from the work it took to draw air in to her lungs. We had not been successful in replacing any of her weight and the near constant diarrhea continued to exceed the fluid replacement we attempted. The lab work kept indicating that her condition was worsening.

"Are you having any pain anywhere, Sally?" I asked her.

She smiled and slowly shook her head *no*, keeping her eyes open had begun to take effort for her.

"I'm sorry," she told me and the nurse.

"What are you sorry about, Sally, dear?" Nurse Cramer asked her.

"I guess I was pretty stupid thinking I shouldn't eat. I brought all this on myself," she admitted.

"We're going to get you better and then we can talk about what you should or shouldn't eat," Cramer told her.

"Sally, is there a reason you stopped eating?" I asked her.

"I was getting so fat. People were laughing at me at school. Mama kept trying to get me to eat. I got so mad at her. Daddy left us alone and she got fat after that."

Mrs. Sullivan as yet had not come to visit, and it was likely that Mr. Sullivan hadn't called her to let her know what was happening with their daughter. Sometime the distortion in the mind of a young person with this disease was so far beyond the reality that she would have thought of herself and her mother as being fat even though in reality they were both too thin to start with.

The following day on a Wednesday, Sally went into coma. She had been in the hospital for twelve days.

The following week-end, I did not have to cover the emergency room nor work in the research lab so I had the time off. I felt a strong need to get away from my work after having spent eight days straight working between the hospital and the office. Dr. Nastasic covered my patients so I could take a little time away.

The Lockhart children and Sister Elaine went for a ride in the airplane. While we were enjoying ourselves on that Saturday, Sally Sullivan suffered a cardiac arrest. Her heart stopped beating. The doctors and nurses attempted the new techniques of closed chest cardiac compressions and respiratory ventilation (CPR) that Doctor Peter Safer had demonstrated to us a few months earlier. This technique was having some success in resuscitating some victims of cardiac arrest. Unfortunately, Sally's bones were so brittle from demineralization that her ribs just splintered. Their attempts to revive her were no good. She died in spite of all of the best efforts.

The failure to cure Sally hit me very hard. I began to despair, feeling helpless and even hopeless, to help the children entrusted to me.

An impromptu visit at my home, from Mrs. Hornsby the

following Tuesday was unexpected. She stood looking as elegant as ever on my front porch ringing the doorbell at eight o'clock in the morning.

"What are you doing calling off work on a Tuesday?" she asked in her chant-like style.

"How did you know I called off?" I smiled and invited her into my home.

"You're not really sick, are you?" she inquired.

I stood there still dressed in my pajamas and bathrobe, not sick. Embarrassed to be caught playing hooky; this was not something I can ever remember doing before that time.

"N...no," I confessed "I've had a rough few days at the hospital. I can't believe you caught me. How did you know I would be home?"

"Sister Elaine told me about the young girl who died and that you were having a hard time with it. She is at the hospital today. She called me and asked me to check in on you."

"It's so sweet of you both to worry about me. I will be alright," my words didn't even sound convincing to me. "Would you like some tea?"

"That would be lovely, yes," she said.

I put the water on the stove and excused myself to go upstairs to get dressed, then joined her in the kitchen.

The kettle whistled and spouted steam. The tea leaves smelled grassy sweet as I scooped it into the pot and set the timer. Papa had sent my mother's English porcelain teapot, cups and saucers as a house warming present carefully wrapped and protected in wads and wads of newspaper. It had arrived with only a tiny chip in one cup. This was the cup I always used. It was imperfect and yet precious.

Mrs. Hornsby was seated with perfect posture in a chair at my kitchen table.

"Is this the first child you've lost, Dr. Aldridge?" she asked as she spooned one sugar cube into her cup and stirred the tea.

"Oh, no," I crossed one arm across my chest and rubbed my upper lip with the first finger of my other hand. "There have been quite a few. From the time I went to medical school until now, there have been many. Even before I started school, I helped the doctor back home. He hired me to assist him when I was in high school. The first time that a child died whom I knew, it was a child he was treating. Dr. Stanton brought me with him on a house call for a six year old with pneumonia. She died just after we got there. I can remember every child who died since then," I reflected.

"That must be awfully hard to bear," she sympathized.

I sighed, considering a response. Yes, it was difficult but I was taught while I was in school that despite our best efforts people will die, even children.

"I've heard people often say 'Parents should never have to bury their children.' That's the unfair reality of life, though. Isn't it? My Papa buried two sons and he never talked about unfairness. Somehow, he just accepted the way things are," I said and told her what Papa told me, "'This world is an imperfect world. But God is Good! We must trust His way.' He would say."

She sipped her tea while it was still very hot. "He sounds like a very special man," she said.

"I've only recently realized how special."

"Well, I have lost five children. Not one took a breath of air before they died. And only one made it through my pregnancy long enough to be buried. The rest died early in my pregnancies. I grieved, of course. It has taken me many years to accept that there were to be no children for me to bear or nurse or call my own, but I have come to love the ones I can hold and help. My grief was more for me than for them as I know that they are in heaven," she stopped for a moment then continued "I'm sure you have been thinking about what you could have done differently for the young woman, right?"

"Over and over again."

"And?" she pushed for more.

I shook my head. In review of those few weeks, there was nothing we did not try. There was no one that I neglected to consult. Only…only, could I have pushed her father harder to bring her mother to see her before she died? It wouldn't have prevented her death, but it could have satisfied her longing for her mother's presence.

"Her father wouldn't do as she requested and let her mother come to see her before she died. I spoke to him but I could have pushed harder. They were divorced and he blamed her for everything. It is just so sad that mother and daughter were kept apart."

I did not cry for Sally at any time before her death nor after. I didn't cry for any of the children that were sick or suffering or dying, except Willa. Nor did I feel guilt for not crying. I still questioned God's purpose for such things and my heart felt very heavy each time it happened.

"I hear your heart aches for this child's suffering. Can I share a scripture with you that has helped me?" she asked.

"Yes."

"In First Corinthians, Chapter fifteen, beginning in verse fifty two there is a promise. It goes, *'For the trumpet will sound, and the dead will be raised incorruptible, and we will be changed. For the corruptible must put on incorruption and this mortal must put on immortality. So when this corruptible shall put on incorruption and this mortal shall have put on immortality, then shall be bought to pass the saying that is written, Death has been swallowed up in victory.'*

"There is a lot discussed in the Bible on the topic of suffering and death, Dr. Aldridge, but death is what most of us seem to be the most concerned about. Death has been conquered. Even suffering will end. We do what we can to help and encourage and love people while we're here. We are meant to do that to demonstrate God's love for others. But more than that we cannot do.

"What more could you have done to get the girl's mother to see her? Did you know where she was?"

"No."

"You can make yourself crazy thinking that it's about you and what you failed to do, but it is not. So, you should stop doing that. It sounds like that particular problem belongs to the girl's father."

She had a not so gentle way of admonishing me about self-pity. I thanked her when I remembered the verse in Proverbs 'Faithful are the wounds of a friend, but the kisses of any enemy are deceitful.' She was speaking a difficult truth out of love.

She stayed with me for an hour or so before she left to meet with her agent about the release of her latest children's book. Her visit made an impact and I redressed in working clothes and went to work.

CHAPTER 25

Joey Stanford

There have been so many STAT emergency room pages for me since that day that Willa came in that I can't count the numbers anymore. Some, like Willa were unforgettable, but on the afternoon of September 12, 1959, a page came across the hospital announcement system that set off events that lead to the turning point of my life.

I heard the triple page "Dr. Aldridge, ER STAT" as I sat in the cafeteria. I put my sandwich down on my plate and trekked briskly to the ER. I took the stairs up one floor because the elevator was too uncertain during visiting hours.

A boy was laying very still on the gurney. I could see he had been bleeding profusely from a wound on left the side of his head. Dr. Denison, a resident, and Drs. Allen and Reitman, both interns were on scene along with Nurse Lewis and Nurse Blum

"Dr. Denison," I addressed the resident.

"The kid took a line drive to the head about twenty-five minutes ago," he said. "Open skull fracture to the left temple, exposed gray matter, unresponsive, hypotensive with a blood pressure of seventy-four over thirty-four, heart rate, 150 beats a minute, and respirations, eleven a minute."

"What treatments have you initiated?" I interrupted.

"We've established two large bore IV lines and we're running fluids. The nurse is preparing a Mannitol IV drip to control brain swelling. We've alerted the neurosurgical team to come in."

"What's the team's ETA?" I questioned.

"They'll be ready in twenty minutes," he responded.

"How old is the child?" I asked.

"Thirteen years old. The parents are in the waiting room," he told me.

I conducted my own neurological examination and called the neurosurgeon to report what we assessed.

"What's the boy's name?" I asked the resident.

"Joey Stanford," the nurse answered.

The other nurse added, "This is Josh Stanford's son. He's the pitcher for the Red Legs. He's just beside himself out there. He's the one who hit the ball that hit the boy," she chattered excitedly.

"Blum. The task at hand, please," the older nurse redirected her.

"Yes, Mrs. Lewis."

I looked blankly at the nurse. I knew that, later, I would have to come face to face with Josh. My mind stalled momentarily but I was able to dismiss my fears for a moment and resume treating the boy.

The child's blood pressure came up slightly with treatment and he stabilized by the time the OR team was ready for him.

It was time to face the parents. I wanted to delegate this task to the resident and I could have done so but I felt compelled to face my fear. With heart racing I went to the waiting room, bringing Dr. Denison along with me. I didn't choose to face my fear alone.

Gloria Stanford sat wringing her hands. The attractive

petite blond woman was dressed casually in shorts and flats. Josh paced anxiously. A mature version of the Josh I remembered looked up at me. At least six other people were in the waiting room with the distraught couple.

"Mr. and Mrs. Stanford," I called to them. They walked over to me.

"Nurse, how is he?" Mrs. Stanford asked.

I kept my focus on her, thinking that maybe if I didn't look at him I could remain calm.

"I am Dr. Aldridge. Your son's injuries are very serious." She gasped.

I continued, "His skull is broken and there is an injury to his brain that will require surgery. Dr. Hunter is the neurosurgeon..."

"Will he be alright?" Josh urgently interrupted.

I still did not look him in the eye. I focused my gaze on his left ear so as to appear to be looking at him.

"We will do everything we can," I said calmly.

"What the hell does that mean?" he interrupted again. I began to feel intimidated but swallowed the feeling down.

"It means, we will do everything we can for him. He could recover but we won't know for a while to what extent he will recover. If he makes it through surgery, he will still have a long way to go. It is unlikely that he will have a complete recovery. He could be paralyzed. He could be unable to walk. He may even remain in a coma. Without surgery he will not make it at all," I explained all the possible scenarios.

Gloria Stanford sobbed with her face buried in her husband's chest. He remained quiet.

"Do we have your permission to do surgery?" I asked.

"Yes," Josh mumbled. "Can we see him before he goes?"

"Yes, but not for long. Time is very important here," I explained.

"I have to tell him something," he said.

"He may not be able to hear you," I said.

"But if he can, I have to tell him something," he spoke just above a whisper.

Gloria hesitated when Josh took her hand and began to follow me. When she looked him in the face she nodded in silence and walked with him to go see their son.

"His head wound is covered with bandages so you won't see it. But his face has begun to swell severely. I just want you to know he may not look like Joey. It is him," I tried to prepare them.

At this point there was no indication that Josh recognized me even though my name was embroidered on my lab coat.

Gloria found an inner strength deep inside and took Joey's hand. "Joey, its Mommy. I love you Don't be scared. I'll be here. I'll be right here. I love you."

Josh, on the other hand, stared at his son; overcome with emotion, he was unable to speak.

I approached Gloria for a signature on the consent form in order to give Josh more time to speak to his son. I got a brief medical history of the boy. He had no allergies, no previous injuries, and only a tonsillectomy at the age of six.

"Mr. Stanford, we're ready," I told him. When he didn't move or speak I nodded for the orderlies to take the boy.

"Wait," Josh spoke loudly, as if snapping out of his trance. He approached Joey on the gurney and leaned in close to the boy's ear.

"You're a good kid. You're the best son a guy can have. I love you. Be strong. We'll have a catch later," Josh's voice was strong for his boy. He repeated "Be strong."

I think he was talking for himself as much as to Joey. The orderlies took the gurney through the double doors and I lead the Stanford's to the surgical waiting room.

Josh stopped me as I was leaving them. My heart skipped a beat.

"Doctor, half of our neighbors were in that other waiting room. Can they wait here with us?" He asked humbly.

"Sure. I'll ask the nurse to show them the way," and I added, "This will take some time. Probably four to five hours, maybe longer. I will check on the surgery often and update you as often as I can."

"Thank you, doctor," he said looking at the name on my coat, "Doctor Aldridge. Thank you." There was not a flicker of recognition on his face. He had no idea that he had affected my life in the way that he had. Here in front of me was the man who so long ago devastated me, terrorized me, and forced me to define myself as 'undeserving,' and 'insignificant.'

Joey could well be in the hospital for quite some time—if he survived at all. There could be many opportunities for Josh to remember me. I chose for the moment not to think about it.

The surgery took much longer than I had told them. Dr. Hunter had to remove many bone fragment splinters that were driven deep into the brain tissue. There was some difficulty controlling multiple small bleeders. Nine hours later Dr. Hunter was satisfied that everything was under control and he had done all that he could. I updated the parents as I had told them I would, being honest but remained hopeful.

Joey was wheeled into the recovery room and weaned off of the anesthesia. I explained to the Stanford's that he would remain on the mechanical ventilator at least overnight and hopefully would be able to be removed from it the next day. At some point, we might be able to determine the extent of the brain injury, but it could be weeks before we might see a return of consciousness.

"My boy! My boy!" Gloria wailed.

Josh, in his own circle of grief repeated, "I'm sorry. I'm so sorry," These statements were interspersed with some profanities. Their friends attempted to comfort them.

I asked if they prayed. The couple admitted that they

didn't go to church, nor pray. Several of their friends stepped up and told them that they prayed and would keep praying for them and Joey. One added, "If you feel, at any time, you want to pray, I will pray with you." Gloria thanked him, but Josh just 'humph'd and walked away.

For me, there was nothing to fear only pity at this time. Joey could still succumb to his injuries or he could be permanently vegetative, or a miracle recovery could happen. I decided I would pray for the latter.

Over the next few days, Joey continued to improve. He was able to come off of the mechanical ventilator and breathe on his own. His neurological checks showed that his reflexes were intact which meant that if the brain damage wasn't too severe that he could move voluntarily. Determining the extent of brain damage and recovery could take months.

Since that time medical diagnostics have come a long way but in 1959, some things we take for granted now, did not exist. We relied on the physician's assessment skills to make diagnosis. Josh was not following commands, moving voluntarily nor opening his eyes spontaneously by week two after the accident.

Joey was thirteen and as tall as his father with a similar build. He had dark brown hair and tanned skin, but not nearly as good looking as his father had been at that age. He spent much of his time outdoors playing baseball, or basketball, or football. He was a star athlete at his middle school and had plans to join every team that he could in high school, including the golf team. Joey was a popular child in school. Young friends came to visit on Saturdays when visiting hours were open for two at a time in addition to family members. By that time, the hospital had changed the restriction on mother's staying with young patients, even overnight, after I had presented a research study demonstrating the healing benefits to the child. Many of his young friends didn't know how to handle what they saw, which was a person their own age, who was in a coma. Most didn't talk to him because they didn't know what to say or felt awkward talking to someone who couldn't respond.

The nurses explained to them that there was a possibility that he could hear them when they talked to him even though he couldn't talk back.

Friends described Joey as fun and easy going. He played harmless pranks on his friends and was full of mischief. At age thirteen, he had a girlfriend, according to his mother, whom he talked about non-stop. Thirteen-year-old, Mae, came to visit him every Saturday. Mae chattered at Joey telling him everything that was going on in school, or reading school assignments to him. She told me at one time "I don't want him to get behind while he's here. If he can hear me read, maybe he can catch up."

Mae needed to believe that Joey could get better and no one wanted to dispel that hope.

One Saturday afternoon, Mae was alone with Joey. His mother had gone home to shower and his father was back to work playing baseball in California. Mae was praying out loud while holding Joey's hand when I walked in the room. She was not dissuaded from her prayers when I went to the bedside.

"Father God, please help Joey to get well," she requested "and hear my words. You are good, Lord. You love Joey and died to save him. He hasn't come to know you, yet. Please heal him so that he may come to know you."

She continued, "Joey's family doesn't know you, Lord. Come to this family in a powerful way. Make his life a testimony to your great love."

She prayed longer in silence, as I left the room, deciding that I would return later to check on him.

Later that afternoon, I returned to check on my patient. Joey's vital signs were stable, his reflexes were still intact and his surgical incision was healed. But there was a slight change in that he moved his right hand to grasp my hand, when I told him to do so. This reaction was consistent, every time I commanded Joey to hold my hand, he did just that. Gloria was present when it happened and cried deliriously at this sign of improvement.

"This is good, Gloria, but don't expect too much just yet," I warned, "Don't give up hope but also don't expect too much. OK?"

"OK," she repeated but kissed Joey's hand and head, over and over. "I can call Josh and tell him, though, can't I?"

"Yes. Of course."

Day by day there were slight signs of return of Joey's awareness of surroundings and attempts to follow commands. His eyes opened each time his mother came into the room.

By the fourth week, Joey was attempting to get out of bed or pulling out tubes like his catheter or IV. We were feeding Joey through a tube in his nose which he needed to get nutrition since he couldn't be fed safely by mouth. He could easily choke or liquid would go down into his lungs and cause pneumonia. Unfortunately, we had to restrain his hands so that he would be safe. This caused him to become more agitated, but his mother could calm him down.

He had to be cleaned and turned every two hours. New techniques in physiotherapy were advancing since the beginning of the Korean Conflict and injured soldiers continued to need rehabilitation. Joey was treated everyday by Physical and Occupational Therapists.

By the end of October, Joey had shown much improvement. The baseball season was over and the Red Legs finished fourth in the National League, so Josh was at the hospital every day. When he was on the road he spoke with Gloria every day for updates on Joey's progress. He was a devoted father.

Joey could not talk but made utterances that sounded close to words.

One morning, as I was walking down the hallway to begin making my rounds, Josh stopped me.

"Dr. Aldridge, shouldn't Joey be talking by now? It seems like he is trying to say something every time he looks at me. And when is he going to start using his right hand and leg? He doesn't even move them. Maybe if you take it out of that brace he can move it," he came close to demanding.

"He is doing very well. Many functions have returned. We don't know how far he will come, though. With brain injuries…"

He interrupted me, "I'm so sick of that term 'brain injuries', it's like 'retarded.' He's a smart kid. Intelligent, you know. He gets good grades in school. He's not stupid."

"Of course he's a smart kid. But it is a physical injury to his brain. The nervous system is very complex. Healing takes more time because brain cells do not grow back. We have to take one day at a time to watch for progress. I know it's slow, but have patience."

I thought this man is not the kind of man to be patient.

He took a long close look at my face. He had not recognized me at any time since I spoke with him on that first day in September. But I sensed that it might just be dawning on him who I was.

"You look a little familiar. Where do I know you from?"

Wishing I could run and hide, I felt tremors shaking me from the inside. Do I tell him the truth? Do I lie and pretend I do not know? Deciding to buy some time I decided on the latter. "I don't know," I answered.

He just flicked his eyebrows upward and stuck out his lower lip. "Hummm," he uttered.

"Joey's incision is healed. Next we need to put metal plate over the place where the skull is missing. The brain needs to be protected and now it's vulnerable to further injury. We are looking at doing this tomorrow. It won't reverse anything and it won't delay any further healing. I'll be by his room in a little while to discuss it with you and Mrs. Stanford," I concluded our conversation and turned to walk away relieved when he didn't call me back.

Sooner or later, he would remember me.

Surgery was decided and scheduled for following day. Joey's head was shaved again and another IV was started in his right arm. As Joey was being wheeled into the operating room, I approached his parents to tell them more about the procedure and answer any questions that they might have. I was assisting with the surgery and so had a little time before I would be needed, as the rest of the team took their places and anesthetized Joey.

Wearing my white scrubs and surgical hat felt like protection but from what I didn't know. The garb was nondescript. Everyone on the team wore the same things, doctors, nurses, and technician. Protection just meant that I blended in with everyone else. It almost felt like a little disguise that covered my identity. It did not work. Josh once again looked into my eyes "I do know you. Aldridge. You're from my home town, Belmont. Right?" while there was recognition there was no sense of any connection with me. I wondered if this was for his wife's benefit.

"That must be it," I maintained the pretense that we had no connection.

"That is great. Someone from home is operating on our boy," he turned to his wife and stated.

"I think it's great that she is a woman. Not that there is anything wrong with a male doctor but a woman would have a gentler touch," she was rambling because she was nervous. "Anyway. Belmont, Huh? Did you go to school with Josh?"

"Maybe we can talk later," I rushed her at this point "They are just about ready. I just wanted to know if you have any questions about the surgery."

Both admitted that they did not so I turned to go in to the operating room.

"Wait," Josh said "Are you Aaron Aldridge's kid sister?"

Oh, no! Oh, no! Panic started up. I walked into the OR without answering to get away, conscious enough of my actions to avoid actually running away. I prayed throughout the entire surgery, thanking God that I was not the one doing the surgery. I couldn't stop my hands from shaking.

Joey's surgery went well. Afterward, Dr. Hunter agreed to go in and talk with the parents about all that was done and how it went. This allowed me to get away for the time being. I was still the physician on Joey's case and would have to face the music sometime.

I devised a plan to start coming in early in the mornings, do rounds and spend the majority of the days in the office, in hopes that I could avoid seeing Josh. Joey was stable and progressing well. Language was not returning, but he understood everything that was said to him. He was taught to point to letters and pictures on a board, to answer questions and communicate what he wanted to tell us. Because of my avoidance plan, I did not get to observe any further interaction between Joey and Mae.

The nurses would fill me in on events. They also said that Josh asked about me every day. He was at times impatient and near belligerent with them about wanting to see me. They were even beginning to question why I had changed my schedule.

One day, Josh came to the office and demanded to speak to me. The office nurse held him at bay while I completed seeing all of my appointments. This didn't help his disposition. By the time I saw him he was irate.

"You are my son's doctor. You should be there to see him every day," he shouted. I brought him into the room that we used for family consultation and closed the door, even though I was terrified of him. Everyone in the office didn't need to hear what we had to say to each other. The little courage that I had came from knowing that there were at least five people just outside the door within calling distance.

"I come to see him every day. Every day," I defended myself. "It's you that I'm avoiding. Why should I put myself in a position that you could hurt me again? I will continue to take care of Joey but I don't want to see you," I said quietly but with a harshness to my voice that faked bravery.

"What the hell are you talking about? I never hurt you," he sounded genuinely confused.

"You can't lie to me. I was the one. Maybe I wasn't the *only* one you hurt, but you took advantage of a twelve year old girl. I was younger than your son is now," I was infuriated that he would pretend that he was innocent.

"You are the liar. I never did anything to you that you didn't ask for. I never hurt you. You're the liar."

"Get out. Get out of my office now," I told him.

"You're my kid's doctor. How stupid is that? You a doctor! Are you a real doctor or just a phony who has everyone fooled? I'm gunna check out your medical license. It's probably a fake. How can a tramp get to be a doctor?"

"Get out!" I screamed.

This was not what I wanted to have happen. Dr. Nastasic came in the door in response to my scream.

"Sir. Please leave now," he said "OR we *will* call the police."

Dr. Nastasic didn't even question who was in the right. He backed me unconditionally.

Josh stormed out slamming doors behind him. Dr. Nastasic told the others to go back to work and then closed the door to speak to me.

"Is that a boyfriend?" he asked.

I gasped at the thought "NO. He..." taking a deep breath but visibly shaking "he's the father of a patient. We know each other from North Carolina. Sort of a family feud," I offered as an excuse so that I wouldn't have to tell him any of the personal stuff.

"We can call the police if he comes back. Are you alright?" his concern was genuine.

"I'm alright. I hope it doesn't come to involving the police. It could be bad for us. He is a pitcher for the Red Legs. He's sort of famous."

"Will he try to hurt you?" he asked.

"I am alright, thank you, Nikola."

"I can follow you home tonight to make sure that you get in safely," he offered. He was really quite sweet.

"I will let you know later. I just want to get back to patients right now. We have people waiting. I am so sorry that this has happened."

We returned to examining our young patients. The remainder of the day went smoothly and I was glad for the routine. Routine included seeing children with sore throats, minor injuries, ear aches, well baby check-ups and such.

We closed the office at six o'clock. Dr. Nastasic did follow me home in his car and waited on the street until I entered my house and closed the door. Before going in I asked him if he would like to come inside for a cup of coffee but he declined explaining that his wife was a very jealous woman. Of course, he didn't have to tell me about his wife's jealousy. He appeared almost embarrassed that I had asked him. I hoped he didn't think that I meant anything by it, more than sharing a cup of coffee.

Things didn't go well after that encounter, as far as Josh went. Things just continued to get worse. He did call the Medical Board to verify my medical license. He spoke to the hospital administrator. Dr. Spence asked him if he had reason to be concerned with my practice and defended everything I had done for Joey Stanford. Of course, neither Josh nor I shared anything with anyone about the past we shared, with the exception of Elaine.

Dr. Spence attempted to arbitrate a meeting between me and Josh Stanford. Josh cited only that his son wasn't getting any better and that it was my fault. Prior to and during the meeting Josh never requested that I excuse myself from his son's case and his complaints were nonspecific. I thought that this was odd. If he didn't trust me, why would he allow me to continue to be Joey's doctor?

During this time, I needed Elaine's support and encouragement more than ever before. She had planned to go on a spiritual retreat and had been looking forward to it for several months. There were some days that she was available before going, and seeing my worry, she told me she would cancel her trip. For the most part, I was able to avoid Josh and so told her that she should go and pray for me whenever she thought about it. Elaine was truly reluctant to leave me especially when she learned that Mrs. Hornsby, my other prayer partner and friend would be out of the country returning to visit her family. Eventually, I convinced her that I would be alright and she should go and she gave in.

I tried to convince myself that as long as I avoided actually seeing Josh, I could maintain my emotions and function as I needed to provide care for my patients but Josh was relentless, once he had me in his sights. He began showing up at the hospital early in the morning and when I again changed my schedule he changed his as well. It was more than just glaring at me or standing over me whenever I examined Joey. He began stalking me and found out where I lived. He showed up at my door one evening, threatening me. I called my neighbor who sent her husband over to intervene. Josh left after he arrived but I spent the night at the neighbor's house.

The next day in a secluded hallway, after hours Josh approached me head on.

"You lied back then. You told your big brother that I hurt you. I never hurt you. You asked for what you got; flipping your long black hair, swishing your hips in my direction. Just like you do now."

The terror returned. Inside my gut tightened and pain shot through my chest. No one was around. He was going to do it again. Just like when I was a little girl. After all this time, he had the control over me.

"I am not trying to come onto you. I am not flirting or seducing you. Josh you are crazy." Speaking as calmly as I could; holding back the scream inside.

"Well, I'm not going to touch you. You are going to make something up to tell my wife, just like you made stuff up to tell your big brother. He almost killed me with a pipe. I didn't do anything and that crazy Indian tried to kill me. If you say something to my wife, I *will* kill you. You better not tell her any of your lies," Josh stood inches from me, intimidating, menacing. His breath smelled like alcohol and he clinched his jaws. I could hear his teeth grinding.

"Why, in the world, would I ever tell your wife what you did to me?"

"To cause trouble. You cause trouble, that's what you do," he snarled.

"Get out of my way or I will scream," still speaking as calmly as I could muster.

"I am going to watch you like a hawk. You better not do anything to my son. I don't want you to touch him."

"Well," I acknowledged "I can excuse myself from his case. We can get you another doctor. Dr. Nastasic can take over or Dr. Cliff. Both are good doctors."

"You're not a doctor. You're not *really* a doctor. You are just telling people that here. You've got everybody fooled but I know you can't be a doctor," his speech was slurring.

"I will go right now to the administrator and tell him that you want a new doctor on Joey's case. I will say you're no longer comfortable with me. That will be the truth. I don't have to say why," at this point I wanted to get taken off the case as much as he wanted it. It would sadden me to release Joey to someone else, but it was obvious that Josh Stanford did not trust me to care for his son and his harassment was beginning to cloud my judgment.

"Fine. Just don't go spreadin' lies about me. Understand? What happened all those years ago was your fault. Not mine."

Josh stumbled down the hall in the direction of his son's room. My insides were like jelly and a cold chill had me shaking uncontrollably.

Within seconds, Gloria Stanford came running down the hall toward me, looking quite frantic. What had he told her, I wondered?

"Dr. Aldridge. Please don't take yourself off of Joey's case. Josh is drunk and not thinking straight. I don't know what he said to you, but please don't leave us now."

"Your husband doesn't have any faith in me. It is alright if he wants someone else. I won't be offended," I tried to beg off.

"No, please. I want you. You have been here the whole time. You know what he needs. You have been up front with us and so good with him. Please stay with us. I don't know what's gotten into Josh. He never drank like this. I think he's just so worried about Joey. Please don't give up on Joey."

Looking for a chance to exit for some time, this seemed like the best opportunity. She needed to let me off the hook.

"Its not that I'm giving up on Joey. He's doing so much better. You're husband just seems to have an issue with me. He would be more comfortable with one of the other doctors. Let's discuss it tomorrow, Mrs. Stanford. Please I need to leave now, I am late for surgery," I lied.

"This late?" she asked.

"It's an emergency," I didn't want to make up more to this lie and I hoped she would just accept it.

"OK. Good luck. I hope the child will be alright. You're

a wonderful doctor, so they are in good hands," she smiled. "Let's talk more tomorrow. Please don't make any decisions tonight about Joey, OK?"

I nodded "Alright." Josh was peering out the door of Joey's room suspicious about what we were discussing. I walked briskly out of the area and out of the building looking back over my shoulder frequently.

CHAPTER 26
Mistake in Surgery

In retrospect, the near tragedy that followed could have been avoided at several points along the way, had I just recognized my own limitations.

The day after the last confrontation with Josh Stanford, I was still very shaken up. The best course of action would have been to excuse myself from performing the emergency appendectomy on seven-year-old, Kelly Murray. But I was aware that my problem was effecting the people with whom I worked. Not only was I asking other physicians to cover my patients but I was becoming impatient with the nurses; snapping at them over minor annoyances. At one point, Sophie Cramer pulled me aside to defend one of 'her nurses' after I had been particularly unkind. Afterward I apologized to the nurse privately for publicly embarrassing her.

The OR room, as usual, was cold but to me felt even colder than normal.

The anesthesiologist, Dr. Mack had put the child 'under' and the scrub nurse and circulating nurse were waiting on me to begin.

"We're ready to start," Dr. Mack stated.

As I stuck my hands out for the nurse to help me don my surgical gloves, I noticed how heavy and uncooperative my fingers felt. A wave of apprehension rippled through me but I dismissed it.

Get it together. This is just an 'appe.' You've done dozens of these, I thought to myself.

"OK, let's start," I said aloud.

Nurses Neal and Warren were experienced, usually relaxed and pleasant nurses in the OR. But my frustration and irritability set them on edge.

"You're too close," I told Neal, at one point, when I felt she was crowding me. Then "You're making me reach for these instruments, get closer," I told her as she placed the instruments in my hand. "You could be a little quicker when I ask for something. Anticipate!" I admonished her.

There were no complications in this patient's condition. The appendix was inflamed but not ruptured. She was average size for her age. She presented no reason for me to be having difficulty .But I was having difficulty.

My hands were clumsy instead of nimble and sensitive. I nicked her bowel with the scalpel and feces leaked into the peritoneal cavity. Neal worked quickly to suction away the blood and material so that I could visualize the nick. We 'washed out' the cavity with saline and instilled antibiotic solution and allowed it to dwell there until I repaired the nick. This is a measure to prevent peritonitis.

Satisfied that things were under control, I rushed to close her abdomen, even before the nurses had completed a sponge count. This process is necessary because a gauze square once soaked with blood can be difficult to see and may be sewn up into the patient's body causing a risk for several post-operative complications.

Dr. Mack was backing off of the anesthesia to bring the child out of sedation.

"The count is off," I heard Warren tell Neal.

They began the count again. The results were the same. One Lap sponge was missing. I had already removed my mask, gloves and cap.

"Do it again," I demanded, as we began looking around the floor, through the sheets, and steel basins of bloody discarded waste.

They repeated the count procedure four times with the same result each time. We had to reopen the wound and look for the missing sponge.

Warren helped me don new gloves, mask and cap. Clearly, she was angry with me by the rough way in which she snapped on the gloves and tied my cap tightly. I had flashbacks of Aaron tying my shoes the morning my mother died.

Once we were back inside the child's belly it took a while to locate the lost sponge, but it was eventually found. Just under the sponge, which was lying tightly over the bowel, was another nick. It had been leaking for thirty minutes. This was a more serious error but I was able to suture the nick and get the situation under control.

Immediately, after the surgery was over, I went to Dr. Spence's office to inform him of what had happened. He needed to be prepared should he have to answer questions on the hospital's behalf. My intention was not to tell him my version of events before anyone else could tell him. If there was fall-out from it I was prepared to accept responsibility.

"Dr. Spence," I began "I messed up."

"These are not my favorite words, Dr. Aldridge," his tone serious.

"I botched the Murray girl's surgery," I continued.

"An appendectomy?" he sounded astonished that I would make an error on such a routine surgery.

He listened to the entire scenario with a few questions along the way expressing concern with the girl's welfare. Dr.

Hunter, the Chief of Surgery, was in surgery at the time but was notified as soon as he was finished. At that time, I was not reprimanded but was excused for the day.

I went home frantically worried about the outcome of my actions, not just what would happen to me but the child's recovery as well. Dr. Spence called me later that evening and instructed me to show up at the hospital at ten a.m.

Sleep never came for me that night.

Three fellow physicians were seated around the enormous conference table in what was known as the Board Room. Dr. Hunter, Dr. Howard, and Dr. Spence had relaxed expressions as I stood at the end of the table.

"Relax, Dr. Aldridge, we're not going to bite you," Dr. Hunter told me. "Please, sit down."

Dr. Hunter did most of the talking. In a reassuring voice he said, "You are not in trouble."

"How is the child?" I asked.

"She did very well overnight. No fevers and her white blood cell count is normal," Dr. Spence informed me.

"Thank God," I blurted out.

"Now, we want to share what we found when we investigated the events in OR three yesterday," Dr. Hunter was referring to the surgery room where the appendectomy was performed. "We spoke with Dr. Mack and the nurses as well as the Chief OR Nurse and concluded that you did nothing wrong."

The relief was indescribable. Maintaining my composure I thanked them.

"Nurse Neal's performance, however was not as expected. Dr. Mack told us that she was slow, that she was crowding you and speaking gibberish."

'Gibberish?' I thought. I don't remember gibberish.

"Nurse Warren also couldn't find fault with any actions you took. And Chief Nurse Patrick told us that Neal had been acting unusual all morning," Dr. Hunter continued.

"Can you corroborate these observations?" Dr. Howard asked me.

"I didn't see anything out of the usual from Neal," I told them. That is when I realized what was going on. Nurse Neal was being sacrificed. She was going to be the scapegoat for the entire debacle. This couldn't happen. "No. No. No. She isn't to blame for any of this. I told you yesterday what happened in there. It was entirely me. My fault," I protested. Nurse Neal could not be set adrift, abandoned like this.

"Now, think about it, Dr. Aldridge," Dr. Howard advised. "Mistakes are made. We don't want to have to discipline one of our best doctors. Our surgeons need to have the best team we can offer them to support them in any situation."

My next question, I asked with great trepidation "What is going to happen to Nurse Neal?"

"Well, she will be disciplined. We haven't decided what that would be at this time but until then, she will be suspended."

"Please, don't do that. None of this was in anyway her fault. She is excellent. You will be cutting off your nose to spit your face. You tell me you want the best team you can get for the doctors, I'm telling you she is one of the best," I pleaded.

"I have worked with her on countless surgeries. She does crowd the surgeon, sometimes. She can be slow at times. I have corrected her for these things myself again and again. As for silly, or chatterbox, yes, sometimes. She is young and needs to learn the OR isn't a place for frivolousness," Dr. Hunter was not going to be moved on this matter.

They had to see that they were making a mistake.

"I am the one. Fire me," I blurted out, without thinking it through.

"That's ridiculous, Rebecca," Dr. Spence said.

"Please. I have been distracted," I confessed. "There has been someone stalking me and it has me just about unhinged. I believe I could be a liability to the hospital right now. I'm sure you've noticed it, Dr. Spence," I said, turning to him for confirmation.

"Dr. Aldridge, if you are speaking of the Stanford boy and his father, I have assigned another physician to the case. Not because you did anything wrong. It is because Mr. Stanford has been relentless in condemning you. You have done everything right with that case. He is wrong but has been disruptive of the operation of the unit and disruptive to you. I think he will leave you alone now," he spoke very kindly.

"Thank you for that, sir. But I am still the one who messed up."

"I want you to stop saying that. I order you to stop saying that," Hunter raised his voice.

"But..." I protested.

Hunter continued, "Not another word. You are not going to be fired. You are not going to be reprimanded. What was said in here will not get back to the staff. Is that understood?"

"I beg you; please don't do this to Neal," I made a passionate plea, but I would not cry in front of these men.

"She has already been notified of the suspension. We will take your request under consideration," Dr. Spence told me.

"Would it be possible to take some time away from the hospital? A leave of absence?" I asked. Not since I requested the continuation of my vacation about two years prior, had I asked for extra time. At that time the answer was 'no.'

"I will take it to the board and let you know this afternoon, Dr. Aldridge," Dr. Spence told me. "In the mean time you may take the rest of the day today."

He escorted me to the door and held it open for me. The heavy wooden door creaked closed behind me. The hallway outside was well lit but cold. Polished floors reflected the ceiling lights but the rain stained windows that lined the hall made it just a little bit dark and melancholy.

An urge to seek out Nurse Neal came over me, but most

likely she had been notified when she arrived early for her shift, that she was being suspended. The urge went unsatisfied and I walked out of the hospital without speaking to anyone.

As promised, later that afternoon, Dr. Spence called me to let me know that my request for a leave of absence was granted. The leave was not indefinite. Two weeks were permitted, if I needed to take that much time, but, he told me that I could return any time before that if I was ready.

Everything that had happened in the previous twenty four hours had me nearly too overwhelmed to think straight. When he called, I had been sitting at my kitchen table just staring out the window at the rain on the trees in the back yard. There was a slight sense of release after his call.

Forgetting that Elaine was at a retreat, I attempted to call her at the House. Sister Laura reminded me that she was unavailable and asked if there was anything she could do for me. "Are you alright?" she asked out of concern.

I reassured her that I was fine even though I was not and thanked her.

Mrs. Hornsby was in France and unavailable.

Once the thought of going back home to the security of Papa's home occurred to me, it became almost a compulsion. I had to get back home immediately. The quickest way would be to fly. Chuck Humphrey from the airport told me that there would be a plane that I could use when the weather let up but the forecast was for rain and possibly storms to continue for several days. The storm front was large enough that most of the eastern states were affected.

I considered flying out possibly in two days after the weather changed but I remained unsettled.

After calling Dr. Nastasic, I packed up my car and started to drive to North Carolina. It was six o'clock in the evening.

CHAPTER 27

A Defining Moment

Driving through rain is not something I have ever been comfortable doing. By the time I got to the twisting uphill and downhill curves in West Virginia, it was beginning to get dark. Visibility was very poor but it was made poorer I realized because I was crying. One misjudgment after another, over a two day period, had not improved with the decision to get in the car and drive 600 miles.

Deprived of sleep for two nights and only fitful sleep for many days prior to that impaired my reflexes, and driving was not one of the things I was focused on at the time. Whether it was a good or bad thing, I don't know but the roads were isolated. Only an occasional car or truck passed me going the other direction and I had no one ahead or behind me for quite some time.

The road turned sharply to the left, but at the speed I was driving, I misjudged the turn and the car began to slide to the right toward the side of the road. The rear end of the car fishtailed and hit a tree but the car kept its forward momentum and flipped over. It rolled a few times but I was disoriented and couldn't tell just how many times it flipped. When it stopped, I felt a pull to my right as if I could fall out of the passenger side of the car.

The car ended up wedged against a small sapling and the driver's side faced the sky. With no small difficulty I was able to push the driver's door open. Without even giving thought as to why, I felt around and found my purse before getting out of the car.

There was a bit of a climb up the hill to get to the road. Once I was standing at the side of the road I looked down at my car. The woods were very dark but my headlights were still on, illuminating the trees in front of it.

I stood in the pouring rain for several minutes, stunned, until I gained an awareness of what had just happened. Since there were neither gas stations nor small towns behind me for many, many miles I decided that I would begin walking in the direction that I had been driving. There were no signs on the road directing me toward a town ahead, either.

My wristwatch had drops of water under the glass and stopped working. I had no idea how long I had been driving or what time it was. The rain came down harder and it was difficult to see in the dark. My clothes were soaked and my shoes squished with each step.

It seemed like I had walked for miles when a car came down the road behind me. He slowed down and pulled over to the side of the road stopping just behind me. Flashing red lights came on and provided me with relief that I was being rescued by the police.

He directed his spotlight on me and shouted as he got out of his car.

"Are you alright?"

"Yeah," I shouted over the sound the rain. "Officer, I had an accident back there," I told him as he approached.

"Yeah! Yeah! I saw it back there down over the cliff. I was

going to get some help because I didn't know if anyone was down there off the side of the mountain. Was there anyone with you?" He asked and he directed me to get into his warm dry vehicle. He pulled a blanket out of the back of the car and wrapped it around me.

"No. I'm by myself."

"Don't know how you walked away from that. Are you sure you are not hurt?"

"I'm not hurt, just frozen. Soaked to the bone," I shivered

"There's a service station up there about a mile. We'll go and have Chuck bring back his tow truck and bring that baby back to the station. Don't think you're gunna drive it anywhere," he chuckled.

We drove on and found Chuck who hopped in his tow truck while the Sheriff took me to a place where I could rent a cabin for the night. His name was Sheriff Tucker Grant. He knew the cabin owner and escorted me into the rental office. He explained what had happened to Tom and Lisa, the couple in the office.

When I pulled the cash out of my purse to pay for the cabin the bills were wet. Several inches of rainwater sloshed inside my purse.

Lisa was very sympathetic when she said "You poor thing. You mus' be chilled to the bone. Tom g'won up't cabin and staht a fiah in the fiahplace for her. I don't suppose you have anything ta sleep in or a change of clothes, do ya?"

"No. There wasn't much chance to get those things out."

"Jus wait heya a second. S' down by the fiah. Wahm ya sef," then she brought me a cup of strong coffee and left the room.

When she returned she carried towels and a clean white nightgown and handed them to me. "This gunna be purdy big on ya but yu'll have sumthin' to waya ta sleep in."

Lisa was average height but plump and old enough to be

my mother. She was kind to provide her own nightgown to me. I accepted.

I hadn't noticed that the lights were out and the place was lit with oil lamps and a fire in the fireplace.

"Can I use your telephone to call my father? I took off and didn't even tell him I was on my way," I asked as I used the towels to dry my hair.

"Oh, I'm sorry, honey. The lights and the phones ah out. It happens a lot up heye. Where's your daddy live?" she asked.

"Belmont in North Carolina. Its just a few miles from Charlotte," I explained.

I continued to shiver. While the men were still out, I unhooked my soaking wet stockings from my garter belt and peeled them off. There was a small foot stool that someone had taken the time to adorn with a needlepoint cushion. I propped my bare feet by the fire.

Tom slammed the door open and rushed in shaking the rain off of himself and his coat.

"Comin down out thar," he stated the obvious. "The're comin' back without yer car."

The office got very quiet as we listened for them to come back. The sounds of the crackling fire and the ticking of a carved cuckoo clock on the wall were comforting against the backdrop of the pouring rain on the metal roof and windows.

Could that clock have been correct? Two thirty? That would mean that I had been driving for eight and a half hours. No, that wasn't right. How long had I been walking in the rain? How long had it been since Sheriff Grant dropped me off at the cabin rental place? I had lost all track of time and location.

"Where is this place?" I asked Lisa.

"Yer in Nolton, West Virginia. Whar did you start off from?" she asked.

"Cincinnati, Ohio. Is it really two thirty?"

"Yup!" Tom answered sitting down in a rocking chair beside me to warm himself by the fire.

The sound of cinders crunching under tires outside announced the arrival of the Sheriff and Chuck. They entered with the same brisk manner that Tom had entered, shaking spritzes of rainwater everywhere. Each time the door opened a damp chill rushed over me. My clothes were still very wet.

"Miss, yer car rolled on down the side of the mountain. Ain't no way I kin git to it with the truck. Kin barely see it with the Sheriff's spot light. You was REAL lucky. Musta been yer guardian angel lookin after you," he told me as he ambled over to pour himself a cup of coffee. "Is it drinkable?"

"Barely," Tom answered.

"Good 'nuff," Chuck sniffed.

The Sheriff took my information for his report and promised to return later after we had all gotten some sleep. He did not seem impressed by my title. That was certainly alright with me. I didn't feel worthy of it.

When the Sheriff was done, Lisa threw her coat around me and took me to my cabin to let me in. The fire was the only light in the room.

"Thar's a oil lamp over thar on the mantle and some matches. Throw yer clothes over the chars so's they kin dry. May smell like smoke in the morning. Thar anythin ya need?" she asked.

"No, thank you for all your kindness, Lisa. I'm sorry to be such trouble."

"Ain't no trouble. Good thing ya aint dead," she said offhand as she left the cabin.

"Maybe!" I said out loud to myself.

Exhaustion made me careless. Clothes lay in disarray around the fireplace. Skirt here. Blouse there. Bra and panties and purse on the floor. Lisa's nearly threadbare nightgown didn't provide much warmth but it was dry and clean.

The bed was inviting. I crawled up and laid down between the crisp cold sheets and pulled up the heavy handmade quilt. The bed was soft and the feather pillow was softer. I wanted nothing more than to escape the horrors of the day through sleep.

Sleep did not come.

I could not escape the thoughts of the accident. The small convertible sports car had rolled over and over. How could I have survived that? Why had a small sapling kept it from plunging all the way down that mountain allowing me go get out as I did?

Was Chuck right? Did I have a guardian angel?

Rain continued to pound hard on the roof of the cabin. It was a sound that I usually loved to hear but now it was only a distraction from sleep.

The oil lamp remained unlighted on the mantle. The fire in the fireplace cast eerie shadows in the unfamiliar room.

I covered my eyes with my hand. Sleep. Sleep. Sleep, I commanded. But no sleep came.

Papa didn't know I was on my way to see him. Elaine was away – incommunicado. No one knew that I had left my home and took off alone. Had I died in the accident no one would have known. Would anyone have ever looked for me in the wreckage at the foot of a mountain?

"Rebecca. I am with you," a voice spoke to me out of the dark room. It was clear and gentle, yet I was startled.

"Who's there?"

The deep shadows in the room could have hidden someone from view.

"You aren't alone. You're here because of me. You're not broken and bleeding at the foot of a mountain. You are safe," he said with a sweet dulcet voice.

"Where are you? I can't see you."

The thick weighty quilt afforded no real protection but I

pulled it up close around my chin anyway. He wasn't making sense. What did he mean 'I was there because of him?'

For quite some time I had been living with emotions that ranged from anxiety to terror. Josh was terrifying me. Also fear of my mistakes, fear of what people thought of me, fear of hurting my patients overwhelmed me.

But, at the moment, the apprehension I was experiencing was *relatively* mild. Here in the middle of the night, in a strange place far away from anyone I knew, and with someone uninvited and alone with me, I was not as afraid as I should have been.

"I AM here. I AM with you," his words were kind, reassuring.

I got out of bed to look around and still didn't see Him.

"Why are you here?"

"Do you know me, daughter?"

"Yes."

"Who am I?" he asked with no particular emphasis on the words.

"Jesus," I answered. I didn't ask.

"Who am I?" he repeated in the same way as before.

"Jesus," I repeated "the Savior."

"Who am I?" he asked a third time.

I was not so quick to respond the last time. I don't know *how* I knew *Him* but I knew for certain that I wasn't wrong.

The dimly lit room became more out of focus as tears obscured my vision. The air seemed thicker and drawing breath was harder. My knees hit the floor.

"You are the Good Shepherd! You are the King of Kings! You are Emmanuel – God with Us!"

His warm hand rested on the top of my bowed head.

"You know me," with three words he confirmed my answer "and you know why I am here."

His presence surrounded me. His voice calmed me. There

was a peace within me that I had not experienced before. He said 'and you know why I am here' but I did not. Was it because He had saved me from dying in the accident? Or was it to give me courage to go on to face Josh?

"Do you know who *you* are?" he softly touched my cheek.

Why was he asking if I knew who I was? Of course, I know who I am.

"Rebecca," I answered.

"Who are you?" he repeated

I thought again about the question. The point of His first questions was that I acknowledged *His* divinity. But how should I respond to the question who am I? Considering the question for a while I eventually answered "I am a physician."

"That is what you *do*. Who *are* you?"

Did I know who I am? I am the daughter of Emily and Jesse Aldridge. I am the sister of Aaron, Matthew and Benjamin. I am sister by marriage and by love of Lorelei, and Ginny, Heidi and Elaine. I am the one who nearly killed a young patient. I am the one who Josh Stanford violated.

"I am a sinner," I confessed.

"Daughter, your sin is covered by my blood. You were washed as white as snow when I went to the cross. Again, I ask, who are you?"

Thoughts whirled but no answer came to the question.

"Why did you push yourself so hard to get where you are?" he asked tenderly.

"I'm sorry, Lord, I don't know what you're asking me," I thought he was referring to the work it took me to become a physician.

"You have been cultivating your pain. Growing it; instead of surrendering it all to me."

"My pain?"

"You have been trying to kill the Spirit within you for so long. For a smart person, daughter you have not been listening to the wisdom of those I have sent to you. I am here to breathe life back into you. My love will sustain you but you must give me your pain. You are my Beloved. I went to the cross because of my love for you."

"I don't deserve Your love."

"Daughter, my love is freely given. I have purchased you with my blood. You believe that you are not sufficient. You believe that you are undeserving. You **are** deserving of My love."

"I am?"

"Your father, Jesse has been heartsick because he sees your pain. He prays for you night and day. I have heard his prayer. Soon I will be calling him home."

My heart sank at His declaration. "Lord, please don't take my Papa away. I need him. Many people need him," tears streamed down my cheeks.

"Don't be sad, child. It has been the longing of his heart for a long time. Heaven is his home. I will be with you until you are with all in heaven. I have plans for you that do not include wallowing in self-pity."

Tears flowed like a river running down my face and neck; stuck for a moment with my thoughts of losing my father. But He was right. Separation would be only temporary. Tears also flowed because of shame. I had known myself only as failure, inadequate, undeserving of love but I had it all wrong all this time. If He chose to go to the cross for my sins, then who am I to think I am undeserving? It would be like telling God He is wrong. How prideful is that? How full of myself to think that I know better than God?

"I do not promise that you will never again face trials and tribulations but I promise that I will never leave you. You will never again feel that you are alone," he told me.

Still there was no physical presentation but He was there. I could hear, and feel Him there with me. Sitting on the rough wood rocking chair I was cradled in His arms. I could feel His heart beating with each beat of my own. Hours went by and He spoke to me of love and what He expected of me. Jesus reassured me that my mother was waiting to get to know me again. He explained that young Sally Sullivan was there whole and perfect and free of pain. Her young life was used by Him to touch people I had never even met. Her loss, as with many things I assumed, was not about me.

The Lord did not tell me my future. He expected that I would be an obedient servant and lead others to Him. It was restating the Great Commission. It was a message that had not changed from before His birth 2000 years ago.

At some point in the early hours I fell asleep.

Gentle rapping at the door woke me and I saw bright sunlight through the cabin window. It was Sheriff Grant at the door looking tired but wearing clean dry clothes.

"Hello, Dr. Aldridge. Are you alright?"

"I am well. Thank you for all you did last night. You were very kind. How are you this morning?"

"Uhm. It's afternoon. Did I wake you?"

"Yes," an uncharacteristic admission for me. "I think I may have just gotten to sleep a little while ago. I must look a mess." My hair was sticking to my cheek and a stray pulled at the corner of my eye. Running my fingers through it probably didn't do much to control it. I avoided the mirror over the fireplace for fear of the sight I would see.

"You look fine, doctor. Doctor" he repeated. "That's pretty impressive. You don't look like any doctor I ever saw."

For some reason his attention made me feel like a school girl. I'm sure I blushed.

"I am a pediatrician. A children's doctor," the puzzled look on his face made me feel like he needed an explanation.

He continued "I drove by the site where your car went over the edge. It's about fifty feet down there laying on its side.

It's at the bottom of the valley, so it's not likely to fall any farther til we get a chance to get to it. But the ground is saturated from the downpour. It will be a while before we can go down there. Since October is pretty out of season for travellers the cabin is available as long as you need it, Tom says."

"Are the telephones back up? I would like to call my father. He may be able to come and get me."

"Telephones are back on line. You can make your call at the office. There's a little restaurant down the road that serves a pretty good skillet breakfast. When you get dressed I will take you there."

"Thank you. I will get dressed and be out in a few minutes. My clothes are going to be..."

Sheriff Grant interrupted me "Lisa called a few people this morning. Gals from our church came up with some clothes for you if you want 'em. Lisa said to tell you the gals felt really bad and wanted to do something to help," he pushed a brown paper bag in front of himself for me to take. "She guessed your size."

I thanked him and accepted the bag, afraid of what I might find but also touched by the kindness of people I had never even met.

Two plain clean dresses and just about everything else I could need were in the bag. There were no shoes in the bag and my shoes were still spongy and wet when I put my feet in them. It was all humbling and wonderful.

It was a new morning. A new start to my life.

CHAPTER 28

Saved for a Purpose

Papa and Paul drove up to get me and take me back home that very day. I told Sheriff Grant that I would do what I could to return in a few days. The weather forecasts for the next few days predicted warmer, dryer conditions, giving the ground time to dry out a little bit. I had telephone numbers of Tom's Cabins and the Sheriff's office and would call when I was on my way back.

Papa hugged me so hard I could barely breathe. Paul told me Papa had driven like a "maniac" trying to get to me. He had to see for himself that I was alright. I hugged him back hard and didn't want to let go but for a wholly different reason. He would never know what Jesus had told me about taking him home. In the years that followed that defining moment with Jesus, I had only told one person, George.

We drove down the road to look at the place where the accident happened before returning to North Carolina.

"I am so glad you didn't decide to fly home this time," Papa admitted. "I don't even want to think about that."

Back home in Papa's house, Jesus was there with me like

I had never experienced Him before. In Papa's church, God's house, I encountered Him even more powerfully through Papa's message, and through the hymns and praises that went up to Him. My prayers had become constant, although He didn't speak to me as He had in the cabin. I knew He was listening.

My bank in Cincinnati wired enough money to the bank in Belmont to purchase a two toned blue and white 1957 Buick. It was a four-door hard top from Mr. Anderson's car dealership. It was a sturdier safer car than the little sports car I treated myself to a few years earlier.

Heidi and the children were doing so very much better than the last time I had seen them. Although Hank had fought child support and alimony through his lawyer friends it was an on-going battle, still not settled. In the meantime, she had gotten a part-time job and had help from her family and friends. I had been sending her money each month to help them out.

Paul asked about Willa, whom he now was very serious about. They wrote and spoke on the telephone every chance they had. He wrote songs for her with the intention of helping her establish a career in music one day.

The visit home lasted only four days and I was anxious to return to Nolton and then Cincinnati to complete some unfinished business. Papa was reluctant to let me drive back alone, but I insisted. My plan was that once I completed what I must in Cincinnati, I would return home to be with Papa for the time he had left. Having no idea how long that would be, meant that I would give up my position and practice in Cincinnati and move back home to Belmont.

The dear woman who had cared for me in my time of need, greeted me like an old friend when I got out of the car in front of the cabin rental office. With her were Esther, and her mother Charlene, two of the 'gals' from church who had given to me from their own precious few belongings. Esther was about my age and Charlene closer to Lisa's age. Their welcome was just as exuberant as Lisa's, even though I had never met them before.

"My husband hepped Chuck git at yer car yestrde," Esther told me "They hain't got it up the mountain yit but they's able to git yer stuff outta it. We warsh'd and arned yer clothes. Din't know what ta do wit yer purdy hats; they's messed up."

"She's such a purdy girl, Lisa. You din't tell us she's such a purdy girl," Charlene declared.

"Thank you, Charlene."

"Ain't you got no husben, girl?" she asked me boldly.

"No. I'm not married," I smiled out of embarrassment. It was a question that I was asked fairly often.

"Well, I want ya ta meet my boy, Everett. He's not married, either. Bout yer age," she grinned.

"Uh...well... thank you, but I have a boyfriend. He's asked me to marry him and I just think I'm going to say yes."

The women invited me in for lunch and we talked most of the afternoon. They wanted to hear all about George and his work as a missionary. It was the first time I had admitted to anyone that I was considering George's proposal. I hadn't even told George.

For some reason, I didn't mention to any of them that I was a doctor. Obviously, Sherriff Grant knew. I wasn't worried about appearing superior, but it just wasn't pertinent to anything we talked about. They had found my doctor's bag that Dr. Stanton had given to me. No one asked about it, nor commented. It was simply set on a small table in my cabin; the same cabin where I encountered the Living Christ.

Nolton was a poor mining town and there was not another physician for twenty miles in either direction. To repay their kindness, I treated some of the children and adults who needed medical attention for the few days that I was there.

CHAPTER 29

Forever Changed

Dr. Spence and the medical board were most happy to hear that I had returned. They were less happy to hear that I would be leaving permanently in one month; the time allotted to find a replacement. Dr. Nastasic was equally disappointed, but understood my need to return home to care for my father. Only two months before, he had lost his father back home in Russia, and would have paid any price to return to see him before he died. But the borders were closed and he was forbidden to return, as he had defected when he left his homeland.

Elaine was back from her retreat by the time I returned.

The Buick coasted up the driveway of the House. Sister Thomasina came to the door to see who was there to visit. Without a word to me, she went back inside to fetch Elaine and the other Sisters. All who were home at the time came outside to meet me and see my new car.

"I didn't think you would ever give up that convertible," Elaine shouted from the top of the steps.

"It's sitting at the bottom of a mountain. It isn't drivable," I reported.

"What!? What happened? Are you alright?" Sister Laura asked alarmed.

Elaine ran to me with open arms followed by the other Sisters. I embraced them all at once.

"Laura, Jesus was there with me. The car rolled over and down the side of that mountain and I walked away. Not a scratch," raising my arms to shoulder level I spun around so that they could see I was unharmed.

"Thank God," one said and the others repeated.

"Yes. Thank God," I marveled.

Later, when we were alone, I confessed to Elaine what had happened to me, from nearly killing my young patient, to the hospital attempting to sacrifice the nurse for that error, and taking off on an impulse late in the evening to go to my father's house. I told her about the kindness of the poor people in a tiny West Virginia town after my accident, and my decision to leave Cincinnati and return home. I told her that I had decided to marry George, if he would still take me and that my unfinished business in Cincinnati was to tell Josh that I forgave him. It didn't matter whether he accepted my forgiveness or not. She and Willa had been right all along. And I knew that I couldn't just forgive him in my heart but that I had to face him and tell him so.

I shared everything, except my encounter with Jesus alone in that mountain cabin. The encounter that had changed me.

CHAPTER 30

Facing the Fear

Josh stood at the coffee vending machine alone making his selection when I walked up to him. He saw me before I spoke. Josh's expression was one of suspicion.

I started the conversation with "I am so happy to hear that Joey is walking on his own. He has come a long way."

"The doctor says he's not going to get much better than he is now," his tone one that barely disguised his hatred of me.

"He will continue to improve, I have no doubt," I offered encouragement. I believed what I said.

"What do you want?" he snapped at me.

Taking a deep breath, I said the words I had been trying to perfect in my head. "Josh we are alone. There is no need to lie to each other right now. What happened occurred a long time ago. For years you had control over me that you didn't even know about."

He started to interrupt me, but I wouldn't allow it. "You may have *really* forgotten how things happened, but you did hurt me. You took away so much from me. Anyway, I have let it go. I won't let what happen to me define who I am anymore. In truth, it drove me to try to prove myself worthy of...anyway, I beat the odds by becoming a doctor. I have accomplished much since then."

He responded rudely "Are you thanking me?"

"Of course not. I want you to know that I have forgiven you." There it was. I said it.

"Forgive me for what? Your brother tried to kill me. You lied and people believed it," he spit out the words and aggressively crowded my space, coming within inches of me, as he had done before. This time I was not afraid.

"I never told him, or anybody else, what you did back then. He figured it out for himself. You are missing the point, Josh. It is in the past. I forgive you. I am moving on. I will not allow you to be inside my head anymore."

Josh Stanford grew smaller at that moment. He had no power over me any longer. He swore and sneered at me, shaking with anger.

"Josh, I think that one day you will realize that what you did was wrong. You need God in your life. HE will be there when you realize that. I'll pray for you every time I think about you. But you know what? I don't think I'll be thinking about you that much anymore."

With those words I turned, and walked away from Josh Stanford.

EPILOGUE

Nearly, twenty years later, I still know who I am. I am a wife, and mother, a former missionary and a practicing pediatric physician, a pilot, and soon a grandmother. But most of all, I am beloved of my Lord Jesus. It is His love that defines me. He has given me everything and I stand on His promise for even more.

The Lord had given me the honor of being there for Papa, to take care of him when he got sick. Three months after I returned home, Papa went home to Jesus.

Paul and Willa married and adopted four children. Paul has written many songs that have been recorded by Willa and many Gospel and Country and Western singers. He has done well and remains a good Christian man and father.

Matt and Ginny had two more children; all grown now.

Lorelei and Sully married and she gave him a lovely daughter that they named Mary Grace.

Dear Heidi struggled for a while but became strong, fierce, and independent. Mitch grew into a fine young man and as an adult reconnected and forgave his father. Lily continues to bring joy to all that take the time to get to know her.

God is Good

ABOUT THE AUTHOR

Ann Szasz, retired from her career as a registered nurse, has fulfilled one of her lifelong dreams by writing *Becka Defined*, her first novel. She was born in Charlotte, North Carolina, grew up in Ohio, and lives in Middlefield, Ohio, with Frank, her husband of twenty-eight years. They share their home with a granddog, Hampton, and a cat, Razz.

CPSIA information can be obtained
at www.ICGtesting.com
Printed in the USA
LVHW03s1217200818
587501LV00003B/91/P